WHISKEY

IRON ROGUES MC

FIONA DAVENPORT

WHISKEY

Zane "Whiskey" Thomas never expected to need a nanny. Not until he became an instant single dad to the infant niece he didn't even know about. Which brought Ellery Grace into his life.

She was too young for him and didn't know anything about motorcycle clubs. But that wasn't going to stop Whiskey from claiming Ellery.

1

WHISKEY

"Zane Thomas?"

When I heard my real name, I glanced up from cleaning my tattoo gun and poked my head around the partition that separated my station from the others to give my clients privacy.

An older woman in a navy-blue pantsuit with a white button-down shirt stood next to the front desk, her eyes searching the room. Considering her boring outfit, her gray hair twisted in a thing at the back of her head, and the low, plain black heels on her feet, I doubted she'd come in for a tattoo. Then again...you never knew what people hid under their outward exterior. The prim and proper librarian in town had a garter belt tattooed on one thigh that Molly had done for her.

"I'm Zane Thomas," I told the woman as I scooted my rolling stool back and stood. "People round here call me Whiskey." Since I patched into the Iron Rogues MC, it was rare that anyone used my legal name except my parents.

"Hmmm," she said in reply, so I had no idea what she was thinking.

"Can I help you with something?"

"My name is Jolene Harris. You have a sister named Lauren Donovan, is that correct?"

My eyes narrowed, and I prowled to the front of the shop. "What the hell does she want now?" I growled.

My older sister had burned all her bridges with our family a few years before. Lauren had gotten into drugs in high school, and though she would get help, she never stayed sober for long.

I was one of the highest sought-after tattoo artists in Tennessee and owned half of the club's tattoo parlor, Iron Inkworks. Plus, I got a cut from our...not so legitimate activities. So Lauren would come to me for money to get off the shit list of whomever she owed that day. Eventually, I accepted that I was just enabling her, but when I cut her off, she forged my mom's signature and emptied my parents' savings account.

Stealing from them was beyond my comprehension. My dad had a rare disease that had fused his spine together and caused him almost constant pain, so my mom spent her time caring for him.

I could take care of my parents financially, so I didn't send the cops after her. However, I managed to get in touch with Lauren and warned her that if she ever came around again, I'd have her ass thrown in jail.

I couldn't imagine what this woman had to do with my sister since she didn't look like she belonged anywhere near Lauren's world.

"I'm sorry to inform you that your sister passed away a few days ago," Jolene informed me, her tone and expression sympathetic.

"Overdose?" I guessed. "Or did one of her dealers finally catch up with her?"

Jolene frowned and patted her hair, looking a little awkward. "Um...car accident. I didn't ask for details. Anyway, I'm a case manager for family services in the town in Kentucky where your sister was living."

Family services? I crossed my arms over my chest and stared her down, confused and fucking irritated to be dealing with this shit. Perhaps I should have felt some sadness that Lauren was gone, but I'd grieved for the sister I'd had as a child a long time ago.

"That would be my parents, not me," I muttered.

"In normal circumstances, yes," she agreed. "But they are unable to care for an infant."

I blanched at her words. "A what?"

"Your sister—"

Jolene was interrupted by the cry of a baby coming from behind the front desk. Her face softened as she turned and bent down. When she straightened, she held a tiny baby in her arms.

"As I was saying. Your sister left behind a three-week-old daughter." She closed the distance between us and held out the crying infant, clearly expecting me to take her. "No father was listed on the birth certificate, and you are her closest living relative, so you have custody of Corinne."

I sputtered for a second, at a loss as to what to do. I didn't know the first thing about babies. But Jolene nudged her against my chest, and my arms automatically unfolded, forming a cradle for her to set the baby in.

The little girl's cries immediately softened to whimpers, and she stared up at me, blinking her whiskey-colored eyes. They were the exact color of mine...which was how I'd earned my road name.

Corinne also had my same dark hair color and olive complexion.

Something in my chest cracked open, and I felt warmth spill out and curl around us. I remembered something I'd seen parents do and began to pace back and forth, hoping to quiet her.

"If you decide you don't want to raise your niece, you can work with social services to have her adopted. However, I can tell you that she has been looked over by a doctor and is perfectly healthy. It appears Lauren stayed clean while pregnant."

I opened my mouth to respond, but nothing came out, so I continued walking with Corinne. As pissed as I was at my sister, I sent up a little thank you that she'd been strong enough not to put this beautiful baby girl at risk.

Jolene smiled and handed me a card. "Please call me if you have any questions. Someone from the local children's services offices will follow up with you since I'm handing the case over to one of their social workers."

She bent behind the desk again, then set what I assumed was a diaper bag and baby seat on the counter. Then she said goodbye and left.

I was too stunned to say anything, and Corinne's cries picked up again. She looked so tiny and innocent against my big, tattoo-covered arms. Carefully, I shifted her to my chest and bounced her from side to side.

My eyes strayed to the clock on the wall, and I groaned. "Fuck, I have a client coming in for their second session on a full sleeve in ten minutes. What the hell am I gonna do?"

"Don't worry, I can watch her for today," Dahlia —my president's old lady—said as she rushed over to take Corinne out of my arms.

"And we've already started stocking up on baby stuff, so she can borrow some things while one of the prospects runs out to grab anything else she needs," Molly—who belonged to my VP—added.

I glanced in her direction, and that was when I noticed a few other old ladies, Elise and Blakely, standing a few feet behind me as well.

Pulling her phone out of her pocket, Blakely offered, "I can work on a list so he'll know what to get."

"Thanks," I muttered. "That'll work for the short-term, but I guess I'm gonna need to find a fucking nanny."

I knew my mom would offer to take care of Corinne, but even without my dad's condition, they were on the older side, having had my sister and me late in life.

Elise clapped her hands, bouncing on the balls of her feet. "Ohhhh, I know the perfect person! I met her last week at the library."

I narrowed my eyes at her but kept my voice gentle as I said, "So you barely know this chick?"

I wasn't sure I wanted some random woman looking after my baby girl. *Whoa.* My baby girl? I'd known her all of five minutes. I couldn't possibly be thinking of her as mine, right?

"I mean, I'm sure you'll run a background check on her, but she was volunteering while she was there." Elise beamed a smile at me. "And I already know that she loves kids because she was reading to a huge group of them. I asked how often she does it because she's amazing, and she's there twice a week. The librarian said they wished they could offer her a full-time job doing it because the daycare center where she's worked since she was a sophomore in high school just shut down, and now she's without a job right when she graduated. A whole semester early."

"Damn, girl." Molly let out an appreciative whistle. "You practically got her entire life story."

Dahlia rocked the baby back and forth. "And she sounds like she'd be the perfect nanny."

"I guess we'll find out," I conceded, looking at the door when the bell went off and lifting my chin at my client as he walked into the studio.

While I worked on coloring in a section of his large tattoo, I ran over what had just gone down in my head about a million times. Was I really considering becoming a single dad? To my surprise, the thought of anyone else raising Corinne made my stomach feel sour.

I told myself it was simply because my parents would be pissed if I didn't keep and raise their grandchild. But I'd never been one to lie to myself, so I quickly admitted that I'd become attached to Corinne in the few minutes I'd held her in my arms.

In that small space of time, she'd become my baby girl, and I knew I would do anything to protect her and make sure she grew up happy and loved.

2

ELLERY

I had always enjoyed going to the library growing up, but it quickly became one of my favorite places when I started reading to kids for the volunteer hours I needed to graduate from high school. Seeing their eyes light up as they discovered the joy that could be found in books made me feel as though I was actually having an impact on their lives. So every time I passed through the doors, I walked into my happy place.

As I neared the front circulation desk, I beamed a smile at the head librarian. "Hey, Lilli."

"Good afternoon, Ellery." She tilted her head toward the reading nook area. "I hope you're ready because you have an even bigger crowd today than usual."

"Awesome!" My smile widened as I pulled a children's book out of my bag. "Hopefully they're all fans of dragons because this is what I planned to read today."

"I'm sure they'll love it."

With that reassurance, I headed toward the back of the library, my eyes widening when I saw the crowd waiting for me. Normally, I had ten to fifteen kids attend my story time, but there were twenty today. But it wasn't the number of children that surprised me—it was the adults with them. And the fact that the man with his back to me was wearing a leather vest with the Iron Rogues MC patch on the back.

Having a dad or two at my reading circle wasn't unusual, but the moms accompanied most of the children. And as far as I was aware, none of the dads who had shown up in the past had been bikers. Until now.

As my gaze skimmed over the group, I recognized the pretty blonde with blue eyes. Elise and I had chatted for a little bit when she was here last week. Judging by the arm slung around her shoulders, my guess was that the man standing next to her was her husband. He wore a vest similar to the other guy in their little group, but I couldn't read the smaller patches on the front from this far away. I assumed he was a biker too, which was kind of surprising since she had mentioned that she was married to a doctor. I guessed it just went to show how little I knew about motorcycle clubs.

When I got closer, Elise grinned at me and waved. My cheeks filled with heat as I returned the gesture, hoping my expression didn't give away my thoughts about how out of place her husband and his friend looked in my reading nook.

To cover my awkwardness, I shifted my focus to the children sitting in a circle on the bright blue carpet. "Ready for reading time?"

Timmy bounced on his bottom, clapping his hands as he smiled up at me. "Miss Ellery is finally here!"

"Yay!" Sally cheered.

My heart melted at the warm welcome I received from the group of kids who had come to hear me read. But that didn't stop me from teasing Timmy, who'd been coming to my reading time since the very first time.

"Finally, huh?" I tapped my finger against the face of the watch strapped to my wrist. "It looks to me like I'm right on time."

"Nuh-uh, I been waitin' foreverrrr," he protested with a firm shake of his head.

His mom shot me an apologetic smile, but I waved off her concern. I was used to Timmy's boisterous personality. It was part of why he was one of my favorites.

I was an only child, but that hadn't stopped me from loving kids. According to my mom, it was part of the reason I enjoyed being around babies so much —because I was trying to make up for the fact that they never gave me the little brother or sister I had wanted so much when I was younger.

Whatever the reason, I just really hoped that I'd be able to find another job working with kids because I found them to be so much easier to deal with than most adults. I appreciated how you never had to guess what children were thinking since they tended to be open books. Like the way Timmy was currently twisted around to glare up at his mom.

Crossing his arms against his thin chest, he muttered, "How come we been here for a whole hour then, Mommy?"

She shook her head with a laugh. "Nice try, kiddo. But we only got here fifteen minutes ago."

"It felt like forever," he grumbled, heaving a deep sigh.

"I guess I better get reading so time will start flying because we'll be having lots of fun," I suggested as I carefully moved through the circle of kids to drop my stuff on the floor next to the big chair I always used. Once I got settled, I glanced up and struggled to keep the smile on my face.

The other man standing near her stared at me with a wicked gleam in his whiskey-brown eyes that was at odds with the baby in the carrier in front of his broad chest. Dressed in a frilly pink outfit, she looked tiny compared to him. Probably because she was since he looked to be about six and a half feet of pure muscle while she was a dainty, weeks-old infant.

His thick, black hair looked as though he had just rolled out of bed, and a beard covered the lower half of his handsome face. The black ink on his neck and hands added to his rough look...and made him even sexier.

I felt drawn to him in a way I had never experienced before, which made no sense since he was well out of my league. A guy who looked like he did, was about a decade older than me, and a member of a motorcycle club had to have women throwing themselves at him on a daily basis. And judging by his beautiful baby girl, he'd already claimed one of them as his own.

Forcing my stare away from him—and clenching my thighs together to ease the ache in my core—I blinked a few times as I tried to focus on the book in my hands. The words swam before my eyes as several of the kids gasped at the cover.

"Oooh, dragons," Sally squealed.

"I love dragons," Timmy cheered.

Their excitement pulled me out of my stupor, and I lifted the book higher so everyone could see it. "That's right, today's book is about a dragon whose wings came in late, so he has to learn how to fly when he's older than everyone else. He's a little embarrassed to be taking lessons with other kids he thinks of as babies, but they help to teach him more than just how to fly."

With everyone's attention on me—including the hot biker I was doing my best to ignore—I dove into the book. But I didn't get lost in the story like usual. I was conscious of him the entire time I read to the children. So much so that my voice cracked a few times while I did my dragon voice.

Luckily, the kids didn't seem to notice that I was off my game. When I got to "The End," they begged for another story, like they always did. So I pulled a second book out of my bag and read it to them too. Once that was done, the kids who were regulars at my reading circle jumped to their feet and raced to their parents after yelling a quick thank you to me. The other children took their cue from them, and then it was a race to the stacks to pick out books to take home, most of which had a dragon theme.

Elise came over to say hi to me, and then she turned to the two men she'd brought with her. "This is my husband, Toby. And our friend Whiskey, with his new daughter, Corinne."

"Umm, hello." I tried my hardest not to gawk at the hot biker holding the pretty baby while my ovaries combusted at the sight.

"Zane," he murmured.

"Pardon?" I asked, my brows drawing together.

His gaze stayed locked on my face as he explained, "My name is Zane."

"Oh."

"On that note, I wanted to go look at some pregnancy books." Elise yanked on her husband's arm to drag him to the nonfiction section of the library.

That left Zane, Corinne, and me alone in the reading nook...and my heart racing. Searching for something to say, I blurted, "She's a little young for reading time at the library, but it's a good habit to form this early."

"Didn't come for the reading thing."

Tilting my head to the side, I asked, "Did you just tag along with Elise and her husband?"

"Nope, I came for you."

That was the last thing I expected him to say... but also something I easily could've fantasized coming out of his mouth. "You did?"

"I need a nanny, and I'm hoping you'll take the position."

3

WHISKEY

I gave myself a mental pat on the back for not giving in to my every instinct to turn into a possessive, obsessed Neanderthal.

Yeah, I was never gonna hear the end of it from my married brothers. And they would hear about it soon because there was no way Blade was gonna keep his mouth shut.

Ellery blinked, her long, thick lashes hiding her gorgeous hazel eyes for just a second. They were almost too big for her heart-shaped face but absolutely perfect for her and so expressive.

From the second I'd spotted her in the library, I'd been able to read her emotions in her eyes and face. That was all it took to know she was mine. But then my gaze had skimmed her body, and holy hell...she was a fucking knockout. The warmth I'd felt in my chest when I'd first seen her quickly spread to my core, then down to my cock—making me hard as a rock.

I'd quickly shifted Corinne's baby carrier so I was holding it in front of me, hiding my obvious state of arousal.

Her full lips were made for kissing, and they were gonna look spectacular wrapped around my dick. Silky light brown hair hung in soft waves to just below her shoulders, some of it resting on big tits that nearly had my knees buckling. They would practically spill out of my hands, and my cock leaked a little precome when I pictured fucking those epic mounds.

As I'd continued my perusal, I smiled in satisfaction. She was tall—although I still towered over her. I'd licked my lips as hunger built inside me when I saw her thick waist, curvy hips, and solid thighs. Then she'd turned and bent down to talk to a little boy, and my mouth watered as I took in her round, ample ass. *Fuck.* She was so damn perfect.

I loved that she wasn't skinny. Not that I had anything against slender women but they just didn't appeal to me. I was a big guy, and I wanted a woman who fit me and wasn't going to break when sex got rough.

The sound of a child laughing had broken me out of my lustful daze, and I remembered where I was. *Shit.* I needed to get myself under control before I scared the shit outta her and she took off.

I glanced down at my daughter and focused on her, taking a deep, cleansing breath. She was sleeping peacefully, her lips curled into a sweet smile. Love like I'd never felt swelled in my chest, and my mind had cleared of everything else.

"Nanny?" Ellery repeated, blinking her incredible eyes once more.

"Yeah, I need a nanny to help care for my daughter and"—I smiled crookedly—"hopefully teach a new dad about how to be…a dad."

Ellery giggled, and the sweet, happy sound was like music to my ears. But then her head tilted, and she watched me with curiosity for a second before her plush lips turned down and her hazel orbs filled with disappointment. "I'm sure your wife will help you with that."

"Wife?" I asked, taken aback. It took a second for me to realize that I hadn't explained my situation clearly. "I'm not married." *Yet.* "I'm single. Corinne's mom was my sister, and she recently passed." My gaze dropped to the baby carrier, and I smiled when I saw Corinne staring up at me with her lips pursed. "Now, I'm this munchkin's dad," I said proudly. I set the baby seat on the nearest table, along with the diaper bag, then unbuckled her and picked her up.

"I'm sorry for your loss," Ellery murmured.

"Thank you, but we weren't close," I replied distractedly. Corinne was getting fussy, and I searched through the diaper bag to find the stuff to make her a bottle. "Probably makes me sound like a callous basta—um, jerk—but we hadn't spoken in years." Corinne let out a wail of anger, and I bounced on my feet, hoping to soothe her until I could get what I needed.

"Let me help," Ellery offered, her eyes soft as she watched me whisper to my daughter and rub her back. "Can I hold her while you make her bottle?"

I mentally smiled, knowing that once Ellery held this sweet baby, she wouldn't be able to refuse my job offer. It was impossible to resist loving Corinne. I'd been her dad for forty-eight hours, and she had me wrapped around her tiny fingers—despite being severely sleep-deprived.

"Hey, sweetie," Ellery cooed as I transferred Corinne into her arms. "I know you're hungry. Daddy's making you some food."

I was mesmerized by the sight of my woman holding her future daughter, but Corinne's angry cry snapped me out of it. I finally located the bottle and formula. After mixing the formula and water, I shook the bottle, then reached for my baby girl.

Inspiration struck, and I shifted her around, as if I wasn't sure how to hold her while feeding.

"Here," she said with another giggle. "If you hold her like this, it'll be comfortable for you, and you can hold the bottle up higher so she doesn't get air bubbles."

She showed me how to hold her, and everywhere she touched, I felt a spark that sent a streak of heat through my body.

"Thanks." My expression turned sheepish. "See? I'm hopeless."

"Not hopeless, you just need practice." Ellery laughed and patted my arm, her hand lingering for a few beats before she dropped it and crossed her arms under her tits, pushing them up. My eyes strayed to the globes straining against her T-shirt, and I swallowed hard when her nipples pebbled, poking through her bra and shirt.

I tore my gaze away and thought about the least sexual things I could imagine until my cock softened slightly.

Clearing my throat, I looked back at her face. "You can see why I need someone to help me? I co-own a tattoo studio and have a huge waiting list, plus any club business that I'm needed for. And clearly, I have a lot to learn. Elise thought you'd be a perfect fit, and"—I grinned down at my girl—"I think Corinne agrees."

I could see she wanted to accept, and I almost blurted out that it was a live-in position to keep her with us at night too, but I worried that would scare her away. After a little more time with me and Corinne, and Ellery wouldn't be able to say no.

An idea formed in my head, and I had to swallow back a wicked smile. My apartment was no place for a baby, and I certainly wasn't gonna raise my daughter at the clubhouse. But I didn't want to pick out a house that Ellery hated since it would be her home too—forever.

I set down Corinne's half-empty bottle and moved her to my shoulder so I could pat her back. Ellery's expression was soft as she watched us, but there was also longing in her eyes.

"Can Corinne and I take you out to dinner?" I asked, giving her my most charming smile and enjoying the fuck outta her cheeks turning a pretty shade of pink.

"To go over the details of the job?"

"We can do that, too," I said with a smirk.

"Um." She cast her eyes toward the ground, and the pink on her cheeks deepened. "Sure. I'll just grab my things and say goodbye to the kids and staff."

"Go ahead, baby. Still need to finish feeding Corinne." I also needed to get Elise and Blade outta here so they didn't fuck up my plans.

Ellery's face flushed adorably, but she smiled brightly before turning and walking away. My eyes stayed on her spectacular ass until Corinne let out a little burp, and I chuckled as I shifted her back into my arm and fed her the rest of the bottle.

She was almost done when Ellery returned—after Elise had already dragged my club brother out of the library to run another errand she said she'd forgotten about. Her shy expression gave me the urge to wrap her up in my arms and hold her close.

I suddenly wondered when I'd gone from badass biker to a cuddler...but judging from my brothers' relationships, I could be both, so I shrugged off the thought.

"If you need to pack up her bag, I can burp her for you," Ellery offered. Her face was soft and dreamy as she looked at my little girl.

"Thanks, baby," I murmured. I loved how she

blushed when I called her that. And that she didn't tell me to stop.

I watched the two of them for a moment, and my lips tipped up at the corners. Seeing my girls together just confirmed what I'd already known. She was too damn young for me, but I didn't give a fuck. Ellery was ours, and I was gonna make sure everyone else knew it too, starting with moving her in with me. Then I'd put a ring on her finger, a baby in her belly, and give her my last name...not necessarily in that order.

4

ELLERY

If someone had told me, even as recently as a month ago, that I would be working for a hot biker in a motorcycle club's compound, I would have told them that they were being ridiculous. I didn't know anyone who rode a motorcycle. I couldn't even remember seeing one up close, except for driving on the street.

But it had been impossible to turn down Zane's offer yesterday. And not just because the job was everything I'd been hoping for since I found out the daycare I worked at was closing. He paid me very well, and I got to spend every day with his adorable daughter...with the added benefit of getting a little time with the only man who had ever brought my libido to life.

"You're so good with her." Elise rubbed her belly, and I figured she was thinking about the baby she carried even though it was too early to tell that she was pregnant. "I wish I had half as much experience with babies as you do. I guess it's a good thing Toby is a doctor. At least he kind of knows what to do with babies since he treats them at the hospital sometimes."

"By the time you have your baby, you'll have plenty of practice," Dahlia reassured her as she pointed at her rounded belly. "I'm sure my sister and I will need all the help we can get with ours due so close to each other."

Elise beamed a smile at her. "Good point."

"I thought I would get some practice in today with Corinne since Dahlia has hogged her for the past couple of days." Molly puffed out her bottom lip in an exaggerated pout as she traced her finger over Corinne's cheek. "But I guess I can't complain too much since Whiskey was really lucky to have found you so quickly."

"I'm glad you think so, but really, I was the lucky one," I disagreed. "I had just about given up hope on finding a position working with kids. I thought I would have to take a job at a fast-food restaurant flipping burgers or something like that. There's nothing wrong with that since it's honest work, but I wouldn't have enjoyed it nearly as much as being Corinne's nanny."

After searching for a new job for an entire month, I started to think that I wouldn't be able to find anything where I could work with kids. The options were slim in Old Bridge, and most places wanted to hire someone with a college degree, not just a high school diploma. It didn't seem to matter that I had worked for more than two years at a daycare because I never got any offers from the interviews I'd done. Not until Zane walked into the library yesterday.

Looking at Elise, I murmured, "Did I remember to thank you for recommending me to Zane?"

"It's the first thing you did this morning." She shook her head with a laugh. "And even if you hadn't, Whiskey did. Twice. Until Toby glared him out of the room for getting too close to me."

Dahlia shot her a knowing look. "Our men can be so ridiculous with their whole caveman thing."

Molly rolled her eyes. "As if one of their club brothers would ever cross a line with an old lady."

"Right?" Elise shrugged. "But even with his ring on my finger, his baby in my belly, and his property patch on my back, Toby still likes to pee circles around me whenever one of the single guys is near."

"His president and VP aren't any different," Dahlia huffed.

"For sure." Molly chuckled before winking at me. "And I bet Whiskey will be the same with his woman too."

"Umm...I...uh...I wouldn't know about that," I mumbled, my cheeks heating as I ducked my head. "I barely know the guy, and I'm just his nanny."

"Uh-huh," Molly drawled with a soft smile. "He asked you to call him Zane, right?"

I nodded, confused by her question.

"Then it's definitely something to keep in mind for later."

Dahlia wagged her brows. "Just in case."

Molly must have taken pity on me because she turned to her friend and said, "It was a good thing you two met at the library last week."

"Yeah, it was like the universe knew Whiskey would need a nanny and you were the perfect person for the job," Dahlia agreed, nodding.

I was relieved that we'd moved past the discussion of how Zane would be with the woman he eventually claimed as his own. As much as I loved their not-so-subtle hints that it would be me, "I just can't believe he's only had Corinne for two days. He's so wonderful with her."

Although he hadn't been familiar with how to feed her a bottle when we met, the man seemed to have taken to being a new father like a duck on water from what I saw this morning. But his schedule was jam-packed between appointments with clients and managing the tattoo parlor. I'd only been working for him for a day, but I already realized that my hours would be anything but regular.

Not that I minded. It had only taken one look for Corinne to wrap me around her tiny pinky finger. I didn't mind being at her daddy's beck and call either. It wasn't as though I had much going on besides my time at the library, and Zane had said it was okay for me to bring her with me if I wanted to keep doing reading time. Which I did, except now I had to bring an Iron Rogues prospect along if Zane couldn't make it.

I thought it was really sweet how protective he was over the baby girl who'd just been thrust into his life. Especially since he told me that he hadn't spoken to his sister in years. The fact that he'd been so quick to step in as his niece's only parent under those circumstances showed what kind of man he was. And made him even more attractive to me, which shouldn't be possible since I had already spent the past day without being able to get him off my mind.

"He's certainly made her a priority." Molly reached out to the plate in the middle of the table in the clubhouse kitchen to snag another cookie that a woman named Sheila had baked that morning. "In only two days, he's managed to hire a nanny and reschedule half of his tattoo appointments. He's also put feelers out for another artist so he can cut back on taking new clients...after Maverick told him there's no way in hell I'm taking on any added responsibilities at the shop. Not when I should be focused on cooking our baby, according to him."

"Wow," I breathed, impressed by how quickly Zane was making changes to his life to ensure he could be a good dad to Corinne.

Molly thought I was reacting to her husband's overprotectiveness. "Maverick has gone a little overboard since I got pregnant."

Dahlia leaned back in her chair and patted her rounded belly. "Same with Kye."

"We only just found out recently, but Toby is already ratcheting up his antics."

Elise shook her head and sighed. "I was hoping he'd be a little more reasonable since he's a doctor."

Molly laughed. "Nah, none of the guys keep a cool head when it comes to their women."

Dahlia shot me a mischievous grin. "Something else to keep in mind."

I grabbed a cookie and shoved it in my mouth to stop myself from saying something I would regret later. It was hard to remember that I barely knew these women since sitting here chatting with them felt like catching up with old friends.

I nearly choked on a chocolate chip because Zane strode into the clubhouse kitchen, almost as if talking about him had conjured him from thin air. Butterflies swirled in my belly when his gaze zeroed in on my face as he headed over to our little group.

"How're things going?" he asked, resting his palm on Corinne's head when he got close.

His thumb was only a couple of inches from my breast, and I thanked my lucky stars that I wore a padded bra today. Otherwise, he'd know that my nipples had pebbled in reaction to his nearness.

Swallowing the lump in my throat, I replied, "Really good. She took a nice nap and had a bottle about half an hour ago."

"Great." He flashed me a panty-dropping smile. "That means you can look at some houses with me online so I can let the real estate agent know what kind of places he should take us to see tomorrow morning."

With everything else he had already done for Corinne, I should've seen it coming, but his announcement shocked me. And even more so that he wanted my input. "You want me to help you pick out a house?"

"Damn straight," he confirmed with a nod. "I'm not gonna buy a place that you hate when you're gonna be spending a fuck of a lot of time there."

My head knew he was talking about being in his home as Corinne's nanny, but my heart couldn't help but hope he meant something else. And that he wanted me to help pick the house because I would need all those hints the women had been giving me about how the Iron Rogues men were with their women.

5

WHISKEY

We were four houses into our search for a new home, but Ellery was still hesitant about giving me her honest opinion. At first, she didn't say anything, then just she told me what she thought I wanted to hear.

Despite being luxuriously decorated and furnished, this place was all wrong for us, so I decided to push her buttons until she finally shared what she really thought.

"So this room here would be a man cave." I pointed at the small living room just to the right of the front door. "And that will be Corinne's bedroom," I continued, gesturing to the even smaller dining room across the entry. "We'll take down the wall between the kitchen and this room so I can walk straight to her crib with her bottle."

"But...um..."

I raised an eyebrow, pressing my lips into a firm line so I wouldn't laugh. "Yes?"

She sighed. "Nothing."

Okay...take it up a notch, Whiskey.

We walked up the stairs, and I wiggled my hand through the opening between two spindles on the wooden railing. "That's not safe. Maybe I'll put up chain-link mesh to close the gaps." I stopped halfway up and swept my hand out over the oddly shaped great room below us. "Perfect for a setup like we have at the clubhouse. A bar, some couches. A couple of pool tables. Maybe some glass coffee tables to class up the place? Gonna put shutters on those little windows to block out the light. And a basket of toys in the corner for the kids."

Ellery looked absolutely appalled, but I didn't wait to see if she'd break. Instead, I bounded the rest of the way up the stairs. The landing at the top had five doors, four were bedrooms and the fifth was a bathroom.

I walked through the nearest door, and my eyes swept over all the cream and dark wood. The fur rugs were a bit much...but then I looked a little closer at the furniture and couldn't contain my giant grin.

The extra-large bed had a canopy top attached to four wooden posts at the head and the foot of the bed. At the top, vertical steel bars filled the gaps between them, and there were restraints hanging on either side. At the foot of the bed, the space between the two middle posts was wider...because there was a pillory in the center. On the wall on either side of the bed were a series of hooks that held all kinds of interesting items. Some I could guess their purpose. Others, I didn't want to know.

Glancing back at Ellery, I had to hide my smile when I saw her bright red cheeks. Damn, she was cute.

We walked in a little farther and realized there was a nook around the wall. Inside was a large wooden structure with several different types of chains and pulleys, along with a brown leather swing.

I'd never been into kink, but I couldn't honestly say that the thought of tying Ellery up or fucking her in that swing didn't make me at least a little hard.

Trying to get away from my thoughts, I stalked across the room to a closed door and opened it. The second I saw inside, laughter burst from my chest. This place was unreal.

It was done in all black...sparkling black. From the floors and walls, to the sink, toilet, and the elevated soaker tub.

But it was the five statues of men surrounding the tub that had amused me. There were two on each side and one at the end. Their hands were up in the air and touching, creating an erotic arch. The four on the sides were made of some kind of dark stone, except for the very long, thick dicks, which were hanging over the tub. Those were painted gold, along with the entirety of the last man. I was considerably oversized in that department, but these cocks were ridiculous.

It looked like there were holes at the end of each shaft, and I couldn't resist seeing if my theory was correct, so I meandered over to the tub and turned the handle on the edge under the gold man. Just as I turned it on, I heard Ellery gasp as a rush of water poured from all five phallic faucets.

I twisted around and cocked my head to the side as I studied her flushed skin, wide eyes, and open mouth. She looked so young and innocent. I'd suspected she was a virgin, but now I was convinced of it. And there was that Neanderthal again, rearing his head at the possibility of being the only man to ever touch her.

Being the only man who would ever know her taste, her sounds of pleasure, how she looked when she came, what she felt like wrapped around his cock —it made me desperate to fuck her. To claim her. But from her reaction to the statues, I had a feeling I would need to take it slow.

I shut the water off, then prowled toward her with a wicked grin. "You okay, baby?"

Ellery double-blinked, then shut her mouth. "Totally," she squeaked before turning around and hotfooting it out of the bathroom. I couldn't help chuckling as I ambled out behind her.

"Well? What do you think?"

Ellery glanced around and pinched her lips together, then marched away from me. I followed her into the hall and watched her poke her head into each room before she faced me with her arms crossed under her tits, momentarily distracting me.

"It's not too bad," I said casually.

Ellery swallowed hard, then tossed her hands in the air and shouted, "Are you out of your mind?"

I grinned as she ranted about all the ways that this place was completely wrong until she clocked my expression.

Then she seemed to run out of steam and shook her head with a self-deprecating smile. "You were messing with me," she concluded.

Winking, I nodded my head. "I want your honest opinion, baby."

"I didn't feel like it was my place to sway you one way or the other."

Her tone was hesitant, and I nearly rolled my eyes and told her that whichever place I bought would be her home too. But I held my tongue on that and closed the distance between us. "This is all new to me, remember? Need your help finding the right place."

After that, she started being very upfront with her thoughts on each place, and I had a feeling that she would have a lot to say about the one we were currently viewing.

I frowned as I scanned the backyard. Although using that term was a bit of a stretch since it was basically a small patch of grass beside a large slab of concrete.

There was nowhere for our children to play. I'd been very specific with the real estate agent when I told him it needed lots of outdoor space for the kids to have a playset, trampoline, and maybe even a pool.

My gaze strayed to Ellery, and I almost laughed

at how she looked around with her cute little nose scrunched up in distaste. "This is just dumb. It can't even be called a sorry excuse for a backyard."

I chuckled, loving her candid response.

"Didn't Zane tell you that we want a big back-yard?" she huffed at the real estate agent.

Damn, she was adorable.

"Yes, but this place has almost everything else you requested," he responded indignantly.

Ellery's eyes narrowed, and I grinned as I stood back and watched her spit fire at the asshole.

"Almost isn't everything, Mr. Chapman. Corinne deserves the perfect home."

Chapman raised his chin in the air and looked down his nose at her. "*You* are not the buyer," he sneered before swinging his gaze to me.

His eyes widened, and all the blood drained from his face when he realized I was glaring at him. Ellery and Corinne brought out a lighter side of me, but normally, I was a grumpy son of a bitch with a dangerous air that intimidated people. "Do not disre-spect my woman again," I told him in a steely tone. "If she says jump, you ask how fucking high, and if you can't go that high, I'll throw your sorry ass up."

"Y-yes, um, yes sir," he stammered.

"We're done for today," I growled. Taking

Ellery's hand, I led her back through the house and out to my bike.

Ellery looked a little dumbfounded as I lifted her onto the seat and secured my helmet on her head. "We'll find the right place eventually," I said, hoping I wasn't lying. Because so far, the choices had been shit.

She blinked, then nodded but didn't speak. I wanted to ask what was on her mind, but I figured it could wait until we were at the clubhouse. Since we were looking at houses fairly close to the compound, it didn't take long to get back.

When we walked inside, a few of my brothers were sitting at the bar talking quietly. One of our enforcers, Ice—a road name he'd earned from his days as a professional hockey player—glanced in our direction.

"Any luck?"

I shook my head, then looked down at Ellery when she tugged on my arm. "I'm going to go find Corinne."

"Sure, baby," I murmured, then kissed the top of her head before watching her spectacular ass as she walked away.

"I might have a solution for you," Ice said thoughtfully. He used the tip of his beer bottle to point at the stool next to him. I strolled over, and Phoenix, who stood behind the bar, handed me a beer. Lifting my chin in thanks, I took a seat and raised my brow at Ice as I took a swig from the bottle.

"Started building a house a few months ago. Decided it was time to have my own space, and it was a good investment." He shrugged and took a drink. "Finished it up last week, but I'm in no rush to move. Staying here a little longer is no big deal. You should look at the house, and if it's what you're looking for, you can buy it from me."

"You serious?" I asked, setting my drink on the bar.

He shrugged again. "It's not like I have a family." He reached into one of the inner pockets of his cut and pulled out a set of keys. "I'll text you the address and the code for the security system."

"Shit," I breathed as I took the keys. "I don't know what to say."

Ice frowned. "Just go. If you say something stupid or mushy, I'll have to break your jaw."

I held out my hand, and we shook, then I nodded and stood, off to find my woman and daughter.

6

ELLERY

S taring up at the two-story brick house with wide eyes, I tried to wrap my head around the fact that we were in front of a place that could easily grace the front of a magazine. When Zane told me that one of his club brothers offered him the home he'd just built for himself, I hadn't been expecting anything like this.

"What do you think so far, baby?" Zane asked, flinging his arm around my shoulders after climbing off his motorcycle.

"It's gorgeous," I breathed, turning my head to blink up at him. "But I have to admit I'm surprised. It doesn't really scream bachelor biker pad, at least not from the outside. Please tell me there won't be any nasty surprises like that one house we saw yesterday."

My cheeks filled with heat as I thought about the penis faucets in the bathroom...and the bed that had left me wondering what it would be like if Zane tied me to a mattress and took my virginity. So much so that I'd fantasized about it during the ride over here and had almost fallen off the back of his motorcycle.

Thank goodness he hadn't been able to see my face when he'd reached back to tug my arms tighter around his broad chest. I never would've come up with a believable excuse while I was wrapped around his muscular body. But I would have tried my best because I wanted to ride on the back of his bike as many times as I could. Between the rush of adrenaline and being so close to Zane, the experience was just that amazing.

It also left my knees a little wobbly, so I reached out for his arm as we walked toward the house.

"Don't worry, Ice has great taste when it comes to houses," he reassured me, pulling the keys out of the pocket of his jeans when we reached the front door. "It shocked the fuck outta me when I stayed at another place he owns once during a charity ride."

Any questions I might've asked about his club brother were wiped from my brain when we stepped into the entryway. "Whoa, it's even more gorgeous in here than out front."

"Told ya not to worry," he teased, pressing his palm against my lower back to nudge me farther into the house.

Huge windows above the door, almost to the top of the cathedral ceiling, let in a ton of light. The floors were roasted pine, and the walls were painted cream. The chandelier above our heads had brass and black finishings that matched the railing on the staircase leading upstairs. The vibe was expensive and masculine. "I could definitely see you living here."

"What about...Corinne?"

The pause before he said his daughter's name was a little odd, but I figured he was just distracted by taking in the home he might be moving into with her soon.

"I'll need to see more of the house, but I can't imagine a place this big doesn't have plenty of room for one little girl." Jerking my chin toward the stairs, I added, "There has to be at least a few bedrooms up there. One of them is bound to work as a nursery."

"Let's go take a look," he suggested with a grin.

Touring the house backward from how we did with the ones we visited with the jerk of a real estate agent yesterday, we walked through the four bedrooms, three bathrooms, and laundry room that were upstairs before we headed back down to see what the living room, dining room, half bath, and kitchen looked like.

"The house keeps getting better and better," I murmured, tracing my fingers over the marble countertop. "If you want me to make dinner while I'm watching Corinne, I'd be more than happy to play in this kitchen. That way, you'd have something to eat when you get home from work."

"You can see yourself here?" he asked, coming up behind me and placing his hands on the edge of the counter to box me in.

Turning to look up at him, I nodded. "Of course, I can. Who couldn't?"

"Then you should move in with us."

At first, I thought I heard him wrong. Then I wondered if he was teasing me. But he had a determined gleam in his eyes as he stared down at me, waiting for my answer. "You really want me to live here?"

"Damn straight," he confirmed with a nod. "You love this place, which makes it perfect."

"I don't know what to say to that," I whispered, my tongue darting out to wet my lips. "Except yes."

His gaze zeroed in on my mouth, and the next thing I knew, he'd pulled me close and dipped his head to capture my lips.

Zane kissed like a starving man, one who was ready to devour all of me.

I'd never been kissed so passionately—or really at all—and it was like adding the sexy cherry on top of the sundae since I had just said yes to moving into the gorgeous house with him and Corinne.

His hands roamed over my body, my sensitive flesh pebbling under the thin material of my shirt. I couldn't hold back the gasp as his hands went to my butt, cupping it firmly before he lifted me on the marble countertop. Wrapping my legs around his waist, I pulled him closer so he was flush against me.

Even through the thin material of my jeans and his, I could feel his hard dick pressing against me.

"Fuck, Ellery," he breathed as his kisses trailed down my neck. "I've been waiting so long to touch you."

Although we'd only met a couple of days ago, I totally understood what he meant. But even if I'd been planning to point out how short it had been since he came to the library, I wouldn't have been able to because his fingers tiptoed down the front of my shirt and then moved their way down to my clothed pussy, dampness already pooling between my thighs.

I've never had a man touch me there. Or anywhere, for that matter.

Feeling Zane's rough hands as he flicked open the button of my jeans and yanked down the zipper to squeeze his hand into my panties just about blew my mind. But when he inched the tip of his finger inside my pussy, he quickly had me close to the brink of ecstasy.

"Fuck, baby, you're already so wet for me. You clamp my fingers too fucking tightly. Are you going to come for me?"

His voice was hoarse, and just from the little pressure of his thumb against my clit, fireworks shot behind my eyes. My whole body shook as I gripped his shoulders, trying to keep my balance.

"That's it, Ellery. Give me what I want. Need to see you fly apart for me."

My orgasm felt as though it went on forever, and I practically melted into the countertop when it was over. Slowly, I opened my eyes to meet his hooded gaze.

His fingers were out of my core, and he was sucking them dry. "You taste so fucking delicious."

"That's the first time anyone's ever done that," I

blurted, my breath catching, making me wish I hadn't said that.

He blinked hard, taking a step back as he placed his hands on either side of my waist.

"You mean to tell me that no other man has made you come? What the hell kind of boys have you been with, Ellery?"

I looked down, fidgeting with the zipper of my jeans, hoping he wasn't seeing how red my face was because it felt as though my skin was heated to one million degrees.

"I've never been with anyone," I whispered.

His hand gruffly went to my chin, forcing my gaze to meet his. "What are you telling me, baby?"

"I'm a virgin," I managed to squeak out, tears welling up in my eyes.

I expected him to walk away right there.

To decide he didn't want anything to do with me.

But instead, he loosened his grip on my chin and gently rubbed his thumb against my cheek. "You mean I get to be the first to touch you? To taste you? To make you mine?"

"If you still want me," I breathed.

"Oh, fuck, baby, you have no idea how bad I want you." He sighed, putting his head down. "But you deserve more than for me to take your sweet cherry on a counter in an empty house."

"So you're not...we're not..." I fumbled.

He leaned in and placed a soft kiss on my lips. "Not here. But soon. I can promise you that much. And this time, I won't stop until I make you mine in every way."

7

WHISKEY

"Where should we put this?" one of the movers asked as he stepped in the front door and held up a blue duffel bag.

It was one of two bags that Ellery had brought with her this morning, after I'd met her parents to assure them that she'd be safe with me. At first, I'd been pissed that she hadn't brought everything, as if this was only a temporary move. But when I asked about the rest of her stuff, she'd shrugged and said, "That's it. I was living at home, so I don't have a lot."

I was definitely gonna have to change that. Luckily, we had a whole new house for her to decorate and furnish.

Ice had encouraged us to move in right away, so I'd booked the movers for two days after we saw the house. I would have preferred the very next day, but I had a full schedule of clients, and I was already gonna be rescheduling the next few for the move. I was tempted to sweet-talk Ellery into my bed that night, but I decided that I wanted our first time to be in our home, in our bed.

"I'll take it," I grunted. I didn't want anyone else touching Ellery's things, especially not taking them back to the primary bedroom.

She walked into the entry from the kitchen and spotted her bag in my hand. Corinne was snuggled into the crook of one arm, looking around with wide-eyed wonder. "I'll take that to my room," Ellery suggested, holding out her free hand.

When we'd arrived at the house earlier, she'd informed me that she would take the room next to Corinne's. Since the movers were due any minute, it hadn't been the right time to tell her in no uncertain terms that from now on, she would be sleeping in my bed. So I hadn't said anything, swallowing all the words I was gonna say later.

I held the duffel out of her reach and shook my head. "Go relax, baby," I suggested with a soft smile.

She rolled her eyes, but her lips curled up at the corners and her cheeks dusted with pink. "I'm perfectly capable of—"

"Ellery," I growled, my smile disappearing. "You and Corinne get your cute little asses in the family room and chill. Let these guys do their job."

Her eyes narrowed a fraction, then she huffed. "You're bossy."

I chuckled and patted her very fine ass before urging her to walk toward the back of the house. "I can be," I admitted with a devilish smirk. "But I promise, you'll be more than satisfied with the rewards when you obey."

The color on her cheeks deepened, and her eyes dropped to my mouth for a moment.

"Go on, baby. We'll talk about it later." If she didn't get a move on, I was gonna grab her and kiss her in a way that neither Corinne nor the movers should witness.

She licked her lips, then swallowed hard before scurrying away.

Shaking my head in amusement, I stalked upstairs to the primary suite and set her bag on a shelf in the largest of the three closets.

It was close to dinner time when the movers finished up, so we ordered takeout for dinner and sat in the kitchen, eating at the large island while Corinne made cute, happy little baby noises in her swing right beside me.

The conversion flowed easily between Ellery and me, like it had from the very beginning. When we were done, she gave Corinne a bottle while I cleaned up, then she helped me bathe my little girl before giving her adorable, noisy good night kisses.

"What do you think, munchkin?" I asked Corinne as I snapped up the front of her pajamas. "I say we keep her."

Corinne gurgled happily and waved her arms in the air.

"I'm glad you agree. Do Daddy a favor and take a nice long sleep so I can convince her. And maybe get to work on giving you a little brother or sister."

Again, she responded with happy sounds and a gummy smile.

"Thanks, baby girl." I'd made sure her room was completely put together before bedtime. So I scooped her into my arms and settled down into the rocker beside her crib.

Small, colorful books were on a little shelf beside me, and I grabbed one to read her a short story. When I finished, her eyes were already half closed, and her thumb was in her mouth. I smiled and pulled the tiny digit from between her lips, then quickly replaced it with a binky just as her face screwed up in frustration. Ellery had told me that the pacifier would be less damaging to her teeth and keep her thumb from getting dried out and chapped.

I stood and kissed her fuzzy little head beside the crib. "Love you, munchkin." Then I gently set her on the mattress and waited for her to settle before I turned off the light and grabbed the baby monitor.

I went downstairs and found Ellery on the couch in the family room. She looked up with a sweet smile when I padded in and dropped onto the cushion next to her.

"You're an amazing dad, Zane," she said, her expression soft.

"Thanks, baby." I looked her directly in the eyes when I added, "You're going to make an incredible mom."

She blushed, and her gaze dropped to her lap. "I hope so. I've always wanted to have a houseful of kids."

Her words conjured up pictures of her with a round belly, and all the blood in my body rushed straight to my cock. Unable to resist any longer, I grabbed the back of Ellery's head, pulling her to me until our lips crashed together.

A little moan escaped her throat as I pushed her back down on the couch. My cock was already throbbing. It needed out of my jeans before I had permanent teeth marks from the zipper.

She pushed her hands between us, breaking the kiss as she looked up at me with those big hazel eyes that'd caught my attention with just one glance. "If we're living together, we should probably be more professional."

"Professional?" I asked, raising an eyebrow.

"Yeah. Professional," she said with a firm nod, though her voice didn't sound quite as confident.

"Fuck that," I growled. "I'm not gonna let you put up a barrier between us, Ellery. You're mine. I'm gonna take you to our bedroom, pop your cherry, and bury myself so deep inside you that you will have no doubt who you belong to."

She gasped, her eyes widening and her pouty, irresistible lips forming a little O.

Grinning, I wrapped her arms around my neck and stood, bringing her to her feet with me. Then I picked her up and threw her over my shoulder. She squealed, and I swatted her beautiful ass, now in my face. "Shhh, baby. You don't want to wake up Corinne."

"You don't need to carry me like this." She giggled, wiggling her body against me.

Fuck, I didn't think I could get any harder, but I

could smell her virgin pussy through her jeans, and it had me raging with need. I was gonna have to make her come a couple of times to make sure she was ready to take me before I shoved my fat cock inside her. Especially since I wasn't sure I'd be able to keep my control once I felt her tight heat around my dick.

I jogged up the stairs to our bedroom and strode to the bed before dropping her on the mattress. She bounced a little, still giggling as she looked at me with wide eyes, her chest heaving, making her big tits bounce with each breath.

"This is your only chance, Ellery. You gotta tell me right now if you want me to stop, baby. 'Cause all I can think about is how badly I want to make you mine. How much I want to taste this pussy and feel you as you come on my tongue, then my cock," I rasped, tracing a line down the seam of her jeans. "If you let me take you, there is no going back." Honestly, I wasn't sure I'd really be able to let her go.

"I want you, Zane," she breathed.

"Thank fuck," I mumbled as I yanked down her jeans and panties, my mouth watering as I looked down at her bare pink pussy.

Tossing them aside, I spread her legs wide, giving me better access to her drenched core.

I dragged her to the edge of the bed and knelt

between her thighs. After one slow lick, she was already trembling.

"Zane." She whispered my name like a prayer, but nothing was holy about what I was about to do to her sweet pussy.

I lapped at her sweet essence, and her hips bucked up, searching for relief. I fucking loved how she reacted to my touch. Hooking a finger inside her, I matched its strokes to those of my tongue, working in tandem to drive her toward her peak. Her moans rang in my ears as her pussy tightened around my fingers.

When her legs were quaking and her hands were clutching my hair with a ferocious grip, I looked up and met her eyes. Fire lit up her gorgeous hazel orbs as she cried out, coming hard on my tongue. "Shhh, baby," I murmured as I worked her through her climax, but when she finished, I still wanted more. I was already addicted to her taste. Besides, every orgasm would help her take my long, thick shaft.

"So fucking sweet," I murmured into her folds. "But I'm gonna need you to do that again, baby."

That was all the warning I gave before I started to build her up again, using my tongue and fingers. When she was about to fall over the edge, I reached up with my free hand and slapped my hand over her mouth, muffling her screams of ecstasy. Only then did I kiss a line up her thighs and pull off her shirt and bra so her beautiful tits were on full display.

"It isn't fair that I'm naked while you're still dressed," she complained, her gaze heating as it drifted over my broad chest.

"That's easy to fix." I grinned, tossing off my shirt before leaning over and wrapping my mouth around one of her pert nipples.

She moaned, bucking her hips closer to me. "More. Please, Zane."

I fucking loved that my girl was such a greedy little thing. I couldn't wait to make her come with my cock in her sweet pussy. To fill her with my seed and see her belly round with my baby.

I managed to suck her nipple while shucking off my pants and boxers, my cock already primed and ready. Then I urged her to move up to the center of the bed before I crawled over her. She seemed fascinated by my tats, and I was grateful she didn't notice how huge I was, or else I probably would've needed to make her come a couple more times before she was relaxed enough for me to get inside her tight, young pussy.

"You ready to take me, baby?" I asked, settling between her thighs.

"Yes. Please, I need you," she begged, her hands clutching my biceps for dear life.

Sliding just the tip inside her, I exhaled harshly as her sex gripped the swollen head of my cock.

"Fuck, you're tight," I gritted out. Then a gush of arousal made her even more slick, and I slid in a little farther, making me groan, "And so damn wet. Fuck."

"Okay so far?" I asked, trying desperately to hold on to my control. I didn't want to hurt her any more than I had to. "Ready for more, baby?" I leaned forward to press my fists into the mattress on either side of her head so I was staring down at her gorgeous face. But once I got that close to her lips, I couldn't resist. Instead of waiting for her reply, I captured her mouth in a deep, wet kiss.

Even with the tip of my cock notched inside her tight-as-fuck pussy, I could have kissed her all damn day. Could have gotten lost in her beautiful mouth so easily. But once she gripped my waist with her thighs, pulling me closer so I inched deeper inside her, I fucking lost it.

I'd told myself that I needed to go slow and take my time with her, but the animal inside me wouldn't wait. The beast wanted to take her now. To go so deep inside her that she would feel me for days. To fill her to the brim with our seed.

Trailing my lips to her ear, I demanded, "Grab onto the headboard, baby."

She froze for a second, then did as she was told, and I grinned. "Good girl." Holding the wooden frame stretched her so her tits were right in my face. I leaned down, licking down to each nipple before I slowly sucked each hardened nub as I started to work my cock in and out of her snug pussy, little by little until I hit the proof of her innocence.

"How does it feel?"

"Good," she breathed.

"Do you like my fat cock inside you, baby?"

"Yes," she moaned, rocking her body to match my movements.

That was all the encouragement I needed to thrust my hips forward and sink balls deep in her heat. Her nails bit into my shoulders, and her inner walls rippled around me as she gasped. I scanned her face, looking for any hint of pain. "Okay?"

"It's, um...I'm...really full." Her eyes were clouded with passion as she blinked up at me, but there were no tears. "There wasn't as much pain as I expected. Only a little pinch. It's just the stretch I need to get used to. You're, um...huge."

Chuckling, I dropped my head against her shoulder, then pressed a kiss to her neck. "Saying shit like that is gonna rip my control to shreds, baby."

"Who says I want you to be in control?" she whispered.

"Fucking hell," I grunted. I would've somehow found the strength to go slow if she needed it, but knowing she was okay meant I could finally let loose.

Lifting her thighs, I wrapped them around my waist, giving me better leverage to hit the right spot and fill her completely with every thrust. She gasped, the sweetest little sound coming from those pouty lips.

"You like that, baby?" I asked, leaning back and moving my thumb between us to find her swollen clit.

"Yes," she breathed again as I circled the hardened nub while pumping in and out of her. "So good."

"Yeah? You gonna come for me? Cream all over my dick?" I asked, picking up the pace as her breathing quickened.

"Yes! Oh, yes! Yessss!" Her voice escalated in volume, so I slammed my mouth down over her to drown out the sound. Her body shook around my shaft as she came, gushing her climax all over me while her muscles rippled, pushing me closer to heaven.

"I'm sorry," she panted.

I punctuated each word with a punishing thrust of my hips. "Don't. Ever. Fucking. Apologize. For. Screaming. For. Me."

She gasped, and her eyes rolled back in her head as I grabbed her ankles, pulling them up toward my shoulders, the angle allowing me to fuck her even harder and deeper.

"Are you on birth control, Ellery?"

Her eyes widened, and she shook her head, but before she could say anything, I strummed her clit with my thumb, making her throw her head back as she moaned passionately.

"Give me another one, baby. I want you to milk my cock like a good girl. I'm going to stuff you full with my come. "

She whimpered as she panted heavily, and her hooded gaze told me everything I needed. I pounded hard into her tight pussy, rutting like an animal between her lush thighs. She was gonna be sore afterward, but I couldn't stop. She was so tight. So wet. So fucking perfect.

I felt her orgasm around me again, and it was my undoing. A seemingly endless stream of come exploded from my cock, filling her until it was oozing out around my dick.

Collapsing against her damp chest, I listened to her heart beating heavily against my ear while we both tried to catch our breath. Once we came down from the high, I slowly pulled out, blocking out the sound of her mewled protest so that I didn't immediately fuck her again. I climbed out of bed, then scooped her into my arms.

She gasped as I lifted her, carrying her the few short steps to the bathroom and setting her down on the marble countertop. First, I gently cleaned between her legs, fighting the urge to beat my chest like a fucking caveman when I saw the smears of blood on her pussy lips and my cock.

Once she was taken care of, I turned on the bath water and ensured it was the perfect temperature before plugging the drain.

"Let's get you in the bath, baby," I murmured as I picked her up again. "It will help with the soreness."

"Are you getting in with me?" she asked with a little bit of sass that made me smile.

"If I get in with you, it will defeat the purpose."

"What do you mean?"

"This is meant to soothe your aches, baby. Help you heal faster. If I get in the tub with your sexy, naked body, I'm gonna fuck you again, and you won't be able to walk for a week."

"Oh," she squeaked, her cheeks turning deep red.

I laughed and helped her into the tub, then gave her a quick kiss before striding out to avoid temptation.

8

ELLERY

Between moving into the house and shopping for a ton of new furniture, the past week had been a whirlwind of activity. Zane had given me free rein to buy whatever Corinne and I needed to make the house he'd bought a home, and I'd had way too much fun shopping.

But once the dust settled, we had all quickly fallen into a routine. After spending the night in his bed—and taking turns with Corinne whenever she woke up—I made breakfast while Zane took a shower and got ready to head into Iron Inkworks. While he was gone, I took care of Corinne. And just in case it was all too much for me, he'd hired the younger sister of one of the guys to come in and clean once a week.

Melanie had come over for the first time yesterday, and I was amazed at how much she got done in only a few hours. The house had already been sparkling clean when I had insisted the sixteen-year-old join me for lunch. I'd enjoyed getting to know her a little while we ate. Her brother Phoenix had patched into the Silver Saints about a decade ago, so she knew a lot about the club.

Lucky for me, Melanie was also a bit of a chatterbox, so she'd shared all sorts of gossip that she'd heard over the years. As a girl who loved going to the library, I had long ago learned that information was power. And being armed with everything Melanie shared had given me enough courage to pack up Corinne and head over to Iron Inkworks in the early evening on a day when Zane had to work late.

He had a client who always came to him for his artwork that he hadn't been able to reschedule. Since the guy hadn't been willing to switch to another artist, Zane had kept the appointment. Which was good because he'd been looking forward to doing the tattoo. But it wasn't so good for me because I'd gotten used to having him around at night, except for the one time he'd had to go to the Iron Rogues compound for something he'd called "club business."

After packing Corinne's diaper bag, I loaded her into the late model SUV that Zane insisted I drive since my car was a decade old and didn't have all the bells and whistles his vehicle had. Plus, with its steel frame, it was a lot safer if we ever got in an accident. Or at least those were all the reasons he'd given me when he'd handed me a set of keys when I had first started working for him.

Now that I knew more about how the Iron Rogues acted when they found the woman they planned to claim, I figured it was proof that Zane wasn't that different from his club brothers. Which gave me hope that he was thinking long-term when it came to our relationship.

The drive to the tattoo shop didn't take long since our house was less than a mile from the club's compound, in territory the Iron Rogues protected. When I pulled up to the curb in front of Iron Inkworks, Molly and Dahlia hurried out of the building to help me get Corinne out of the vehicle.

"Oh my goodness," Molly squealed as she peered into the baby carrier. "It's not even been a week since I've seen this sweet little one, but it looks like she's already grown up so much in such a short time."

"Look at her hair," Dahlia sighed, leaning in from the other side of the SUV. "It's at least an inch longer. And those curls."

"She's barely grown at all, and it's only been a

few days since we hung out at the clubhouse with her." Gently nudging Molly out of my way, I pulled the baby carrier out of the back seat. Dahlia grabbed the diaper bag before I could reach for it.

"Can you blame us for being baby crazy?" Molly asked with a sheepish grin.

Dahlia circled the vehicle and pointed at her rounded belly. "Yeah, we have all the pregnancy hormones roaring through our bodies right now."

"You don't have too much longer before you can't use that excuse anymore," I chided, shaking my head with a laugh.

"True," Molly conceded, her smile widening. "Which is why we have to take advantage of it while we still can."

"Then we can switch to exhaustion and mommy brain as our new excuses," Dahlia added with a giggle.

"Yes," Molly cheered. "And I'm sure we'll come up with something else after that."

Dahlia rolled her eyes. "Yeah, probably another pregnancy, knowing our men."

"Yup," Molly agreed as we walked into the tattoo shop.

As hilarious as Molly and Dahlia were, my focus immediately shifted to the man standing beside the reception desk. His lips curved into a huge smile when he spotted me. "Hey, baby. I didn't know you were gonna stop by today."

"I know. I wanted to surprise you."

I heard a soft "aw" behind me, but I was too busy staring at Zane as he strode toward me to see which sister had said it.

"My favorite kind of surprise," he murmured, bending his head to give me a kiss when he got near.

Then he took the baby carrier from me, and I turned to grab the diaper bag from Dahlia. "I also brought dinner."

"Careful, baby, or you're gonna spoil me," he warned with a grin.

I returned his smile before digging in the bag for the container of spaghetti and meatballs big enough to feed an army. "Only because you deserve it with how much you spoil me."

"Yum," Molly hummed as she came to my side to peer at the food. "Did you bring enough for Whiskey to share?"

"Of course, I did," I confirmed with a laugh. "I know better than to bring dinner without having anything for the two pregnant women here."

"Smart." Dahlia winked at me. "It saves us from

having to call our men to tattle on yours for starving us."

Zane glanced over my shoulder, his lips pressing together as his gaze returned to me. "Where's the prospect?"

"Sorry." I flashed him an apologetic smile. "I figured since I was coming to see you that I didn't need to ask him to drive over just to turn around and follow me in the same direction he'd come from."

"You don't need to worry about inconveniencing a prospect. That's the whole point of the time they spend earning their patch. Text him next time," he growled.

"See?" Molly mouthed, pointing at Zane. "Neanderthal."

Rolling my eyes, I dished up the pasta for everyone, smiling as they dug right in. Zane had just finished up and was taking care of something in the back when his client walked in. Molly and Dahlia greeted him, but the guy's gaze zeroed in on me.

"Hey." He flashed me a smile. "You must be new. I'm Dirk. One of Whiskey's very best clients, so you'll be seeing a lot of me."

"Um, hi. Sorry, but I don't work here," I mumbled.

"Are you getting a tattoo from Molly?" he asked.

"I can help you pick out where to put it since I have a ton of 'em."

"Unless you want me to cut off all the art I've put on your skin, you'd better get the fuck away from my woman," Zane growled as he prowled into the waiting area.

Dirk's eyes widened, and he jumped back a few steps, raising his hands in the air in a gesture of surrender. "Sorry, man. I had no idea she was yours."

"Maybe you shoulda used your brain instead of thinking with your dick." Zane glared at him as he wrapped his arm around my shoulders. "You ever see a woman in a place owned by the Iron Rogues, assume she belongs to one of us."

"Sorry. Like I said, I didn't know." He shook his head with a sigh. "If I had, I never would've hit on her."

Glancing at Molly and Dahlia, I couldn't help but think that we wouldn't have been in this situation if Zane had given me a vest like they wore. A property patch proclaiming me as Whiskey's would have made it pretty darn clear to any man who saw me that an Iron Rogue had claimed me. Hopefully, I would wear it someday soon.

9

WHISKEY

"I'm nervous," Ellery whispered.

Her hand was clasped in mine, resting on my thigh, so I gave it a gentle squeeze. "Don't be. They're gonna love you, baby."

I was taking my girls home to see my parents. They'd already spent a little time with Corinne, but not much because of everything going on, between trying to get settled and figuring out our routine.

Telling them about Laura had been hard and despite all she'd done, they were still understandably devastated to hear that their daughter was dead. But Corinne had helped to heal them. Even if she hadn't been their biological granddaughter, no one could meet my baby girl and not fall in love with her.

When I told my mom about Ellery, she'd begged

me to bring her to meet them. It had taken a little time and a whole lot of orgasms to convince my girl, but she'd finally agreed.

I stopped at a red light and glanced over at her just as the baby let out a little cry. Ellery's lips formed a sexy little pout, making me want to bite them. "See? Even Corinne thinks this is a bad idea."

A laugh rumbled in my chest, and I shook my head. "Relax, baby. I'm pretty sure that smell coming from the back is why Corinne is fussing."

Ellery sighed. "Probably."

Luckily, we didn't have to endure the odor for long because I pulled into my parents' driveway a couple of minutes later.

My mom came barging out of the house and went straight to the back of the car, wrenching the door open. "Hello, my sweet little grandbaby! How are you, cutie? Did you miss Grandma?" She chattered on as she unbuckled the baby and lifted her out of the car seat, then cradled her against her chest.

I opened the car door and climbed out, rolling my eyes when my mom didn't even acknowledge me as I slammed it shut behind me. I muttered as I rounded the hood of the car and opened Ellery's door, then helped her out of her seat.

My mom finally looked up from the baby. "My

goodness," she exclaimed. "Look at how gorgeous you are!"

Ellery's cheeks heated, but she smiled shyly back at my mom. "Um, thank you."

"Hey, Mom," I grumbled. "Nice to see you, too."

"Oh pish, Zane," she muttered, looking back down at the baby. "You know I'm always happy to see my boy. Now, introduce me to your girl."

"Mom, this is my Ellery. Baby, this is my mom, Diana. Don't believe any stories she tells you about me. She lies."

Mom gasped and tossed me an indignant glare.

"Nice to meet you, Mrs. Thomas," Ellery said sweetly, even as she elbowed me in the ribs and whispered, "Be nice."

My mom grinned widely. "Well, aren't you all sugar and spice? I have a feeling we're going to get along wonderfully!" She held Corinne with one arm and slipped the other through Ellery's before leading her toward the house. "Come, come. Dinner is almost ready!"

My dad, who looked like an older version of me, stood at the door, grinning widely. His body was slightly hunched, and he walked a little stiffly when he moved back to let us enter, but his whiskey-colored eyes twinkled. Despite being in constant pain, my dad was one of the most upbeat and opti-mistic people I knew.

"Dad, this is Ellery."

"Nice to finally meet the girl we've heard so much about," he said as he took Ellery's hand.

"*My* girl," I grunted, snatching her hand back and tucking her under my arm. It was ridiculous, but I couldn't seem to control my caveman instincts around Ellery.

She rolled her eyes and peered up at me. "He's your father, for Pete's sake."

I just shrugged and led her through the house, ignoring the laughter following me. When we reached the kitchen, I set Corinne's diaper bag on the counter. Then I leaned against it and pulled Ellery to me so she stood between my legs, her back to my front. "Anything I can help with?" I asked as I rested my chin on Ellery's head.

"You can set the table," my mom instructed distractedly as she cooed at Corinne. A timer went off, and she sighed, making me chuckle. "I'd better get dinner out of the oven."

Reluctantly, I let Ellery go when she reached for Corinne. As usual, as soon as my baby girl was in Ellery's arms, she snuggled in close and relaxed. Warmth spread through my chest as I watched my girls until my mom snapped a dish towel on my arm. "Son of a bitch!" I muttered.

"Watch your language, young man," my mom admonished with a glare. "Now, get the table set."

Ellery giggled, and I couldn't help smiling at the sound, but I pretended to grumble as I walked to the cupboard to grab plates.

"I'm going to change Corinne and make a bottle," she told me softly.

"Thanks, baby." I planted a kiss on her lips as I walked by.

She gasped before her eyes darted around, then landed back on me. "You can't kiss me in front of your parents," she hissed.

"The hell I can't," I growled before slipping an arm around her waist and hauling her body into mine. My mouth covered hers, and I gave her a hard, intense kiss. When I pulled back, she looked dazed, and I couldn't help smirking. "You're mine. I'll kiss you whenever I damn well please." I patted her sexy ass, then let her go and moseyed out to the dining room.

"Just like his father," my mom muttered.

My dad laughed, and I glanced up as he walked into the room. He had the silverware, and for a few moments, we completed our task in silence. When we'd added everything else to the table, we re-entered the kitchen, and he grabbed us both a beer from the fridge.

"When is the wedding?" he asked with a sly grin.

"When do I get more grandbabies?" my mom piped up.

I took a drink from my bottle, then grinned. "Soon."

Ellery returned before I could say anything else, and my mom announced that everything was ready. She asked to feed Corinne, so Ellery gently passed her over before taking her seat next to me.

During the meal, my parents got to know my girl and entertained her with ridiculous stories from my childhood. It didn't escape my notice that none of them included Laura, and I was grateful for that. Ellery and I had talked about my sister, so it wasn't like she would be blindsided by the mention, but it was still a raw subject for me and my parents.

Corinne had fallen asleep after her bottle, so we put her in her baby carrier and set her in my old bedroom. My parents had bought a baby monitor after the first time I brought her to see them.

It was an unseasonably warm night in January, even for southern Tennessee, so we took the monitor with us outside and built a fire in the pit on my parents' porch. We continued to talk and laugh, and my parents even broke out the fixings for s'mores. Ellery fit perfectly with my family, as if we'd carved out a spot for her and had been waiting for her to fill it.

Waiting to get my ring on her drove me crazy, but Sheila—the old lady who usually handled the property vests—and her old man had been on vacation and wouldn't be back for another week. I wanted to wait to propose until she was wearing my property patch.

Not that those things had stopped me from trying to knock her up already.

When the fire died down, it was getting late, and I had an early client. Not to mention that we would be up with Corinne a couple more times in the night. So we packed up the car, got our little one, and said our goodbyes.

"I expect my son to bring you back very soon," my mom told Ellery as she held her face in her hands. "Heck, you don't need to wait for him. Come see me anytime, beautiful." Then she kissed my girl's cheeks before letting her go.

While Ellery spoke with my dad, my mom came over to hug me. "I couldn't have chosen anyone more perfect for you, Zane. She's special. Don't let her go, or I'll disown you and adopt her."

I pretended to look offended, but then I laughed and shook my head. "I would do the same thing in your shoes."

Once we were in the car and headed home, I laced my fingers through Ellery's and rested our joint hands on my thigh. "Told you they'd love you," I said smugly.

"Your parents are awesome." She giggled and added, "They are so cute when they get all mushy over Corinne. Especially your dad."

"Yeah. It's hard to believe that anyone could treat them like Laura did," I muttered bitterly.

Ellery squeezed my hand gently. "She was sick, Zane."

Sighing, I brought her hand to my lips and kissed the back. "I know, baby. And I'll make my peace with her eventually, if for no other reason than because of Corinne."

"You're a good man," Ellery whispered.

"I wouldn't go that far, baby. In fact, when we get home, I'm gonna show you just how bad I can be."

L iving with Zane and Corinne was a dream, but I couldn't help but worry about how difficult it would be to leave them if my relationship ended. I'd never had a boyfriend before, let alone whatever you'd call a man like Zane.

Partner? Lover?

Either way, he hadn't said anything about love or marriage yet, and I was scared he would get bored with me at some point in the future. And where would I be then? Stuck without a job or home and moving back into my parents' house.

As happy as I was with him, I needed to protect myself from that being my future. Which was why I'd looked at the job openings in town while he was at Iron Inkworks today.

"You know there's a new daycare opening up just north of here," I said as we started back down the stairs now that Corinne was finally asleep for the night.

Zane frowned, turning toward me just as I got off the bottom step. "You mean that one that's off Thirty? Almost an hour from here?"

I tilted my head. "Yeah, I guess it's about that far. Anyway, I saw that they were hiring, and since I have experience, I thought it could be good to get something part-time. You know, as a backup."

"A backup? For what?" He folded his arms across his broad chest, pulling his shirt tighter as the veins in his biceps bulged beneath his tattoos.

Biting my bottom lip, I looked down at the hardwood floor beneath my feet, tracing the lines of the plank with my shoe.

There was no easy way to say that I was worried we would eventually break up. Especially not when things were going so well between us. The last thing I wanted was to pick a fight with Zane.

"Corinne isn't going to need someone to take care of her forever," I said, still looking down.

He laughed. "Well, then you'll have your hands full when our kids start coming."

I shot my head up, meeting his bright smile. "Our kids? What kids?"

"Like the one you could be carrying right now."

We'd had sex every night for the past week, yet I'd somehow never once thought about birth control. But it sounded as though he was aware of the oversight...but not concerned. "Whoa, I could be pregnant."

He leaned in closer, the whiskers of his beard tickling my chin as he whispered, "And if you're not, I'm going to fuck you every chance I get until you are."

It would have been so easy to think he was teasing, except his arms wrapped around my waist and he lifted me like I was nothing, tossing me over his shoulder before barreling back upstairs toward the bedroom we shared.

I giggled despite his heated words and what they were definitely doing to me. I'd always wanted a big family, and to know he wanted one too was enough to warm a girl's heart.

And more.

He kicked the door closed behind us before tossing me on the mattress, wasting no time pawing at my jeans and tossing them aside with my panties.

"I've been thinking about tasting this sweet pussy

all day," he moaned before kneeling between my legs and licking a long line up my core.

Leaning back on the pillows, I put my hands on his head, spreading my legs wider and giving him better access to my already wet and waiting pussy. He dove in, his heated gaze like on mine as his tongue lapped up every bit of me.

"Yes, Zane. Right there," I moaned, leaning back as desire pooled low in my belly.

"Look at me when I make you come, Ellery. I want you to watch," he growled between my thighs.

My gaze shot back to his as he sucked hard on my clit, making fireworks blast through every part of me as my body shook.

He grinned, lapping up every bit of my come as aftershocks rolled through me. Then he kissed a trail up my thighs before getting to his knees.

I gawked up at him as he ripped off his clothes before his lips met mine again. At some point, my bra and shirt were thrown by the wayside, but all I could focus on was his tongue devouring mine. My own sweet saltiness on his lips and the way he growled as he pressed the hard lines of his body against me.

"Are you ready for me to fill this tight pussy?" he murmured, sliding his hands between us, running his thick fingers along my swollen clit.

"Yes, please," I begged, pushing my hips closer to his waiting hand.

"That's my good girl," he said through a laugh as he plunged two fingers deep inside my waiting pussy. "Because I'm going to keep fucking this pussy every chance I get. And I'm going to fill it with my come until your belly is round with my baby. Then I'm going to keep fucking this beautiful body. Do you want that, baby? Do you want me to make you mine?"

"Yes, please," I whimpered, another orgasm already building up on his fingers.

It wasn't just the way he was touching me that was shoving me close to the edge again.

My heart swelled at his words because the picture he painted was everything I'd ever wanted.

A beautiful house.

A family.

A man who I adored.

It was perfect.

As my orgasm crested, I kept my eyes open, meeting Zane's hooded gaze as he took me over the edge again.

"Fuck, baby." He pulled his fingers out of me and then pressed the wet tips against my lips.

"Taste yourself. Taste what you made for me."

I tentatively darted out my tongue, licking the saltiness from his fingers before gripping his thumb and taking both fingers as far as they could go into my mouth, gagging as they hit the back of my throat.

"Fuck, baby, that's so hot." He gripped the back of my neck with his free hand. "And as much as I want those lips wrapped around my cock and have you gagging until your eyes water, we've got some babies to make."

Pulling his fingers out with a pop, he kissed my lips hard, his cock already hard and ready as he slowly dipped into my wet folds. Each inch was more exquisite than the last, and I moaned deeply once he filled me to the hilt.

He closed his eyes, slowly grinding against me. "Fuck, you're so hot. So wet. You feel fucking amazing."

"You too," I managed to breathe as I gripped the strong muscles of his back.

"You take my cock so well. Look at it. Look how fucking hot this pussy looks, filled with me," he said, opening his eyes and looking between us.

His cock was slick with my juices, sliding slowly in and out of me. But even hotter was the lusty gaze on his face as he watched.

"So hot," I murmured.

He picked up the pace, propping up on one elbow while his other hand went between us. Then his thumb circled my clit in the same fast rhythm he fucked my drenched pussy.

"Oh, yes, Zane. I'm going to come again," I warned.

"Yes, baby, come for me. Open up so I can fill you up with my come."

Spreading my legs wider, my entire body shook as my orgasm took hold.

"Fuck," he groaned, pumping faster and following soon after me, his come shooting out in hot spurts as he filled me.

We both lay there momentarily, catching our breath as he peppered kisses along my chest and stomach. Then as his dick slid out of me, he pushed two fingers back inside, slowly swirling them around my wet pussy.

"What are you doing?" I asked, sitting up on my elbows.

He grinned. "Gotta make sure my seed is in there. Who knows? Maybe we can have twins right off the bat."

I wanted to laugh, but another orgasm quickly took hold, and I let out a low moan, shaking around his fingers.

"You're so fucking hot when you come for me, baby. I love it."

And I love you, I thought to myself as my eyelids drifted shut, totally wiped between all of the mind-blowing orgasms and waking up with Corinne twice last night. I wasn't quite ready to say those three little words out loud yet, but I felt more confident that Zane was feeling the same way after he'd shared his plans to make a family with me...and followed that up with doing his best to try to get me pregnant.

11

WHISKEY

"I'm looking for Zane Thomas."

I was working in the office when I heard someone asking for me. My next client wasn't for another hour, and just about anyone who came here looking for me would have asked for Whiskey.

Curious, I stood from the desk and was already walking out of my office when Dahlia answered him.

"Do you have an appointment?" She was well aware that he didn't, so she was fishing for information.

Seeing as how MCs usually adhered to our own brand of justice, we sometimes worked outside the laws of the land. So strangers were always regarded with suspicion until they proved themselves. It was a big part of why we only worked on referral, another reason anyone asking for me wouldn't be using my given name.

The man wore jeans and a wrinkled T-shirt with a logo so faded I couldn't make it out. His hair was greasy, he had a day's worth of growth on his face, and his eyes...they were a little glassy and his pupils were dilated. *Shit.* The fucker was high.

"Who the fuck are you?" I growled as I ambled up to the counter to stand next to Dahlia. I gently pushed her behind me and stood in a wide stance with my arms crossed over my chest.

The man's eyes landed on my tatted biceps, and he swallowed hard. But the drugs must have given him courage because he lifted his chin and glared at me.

"I'm Kenny. I'm here for my daughter."

"The fuck?" I snapped.

"You have my baby. Laura's baby. I'm her father."

I took a menacing step forward, and he gulped but stood his ground.

"The fuck you are," I snarled, my scowl causing him to back up a step. "There was no father listed on the birth certificate."

"Well...uh...Laura and I had a...uh, falling out. And she was just being a bitch—"

Before he could say anything else, I was around the desk and had my hand around his throat. "Think very hard about what you say next, asshole."

Since he couldn't talk while I was choking him, I eased up my grip.

"She was mad at me, okay? I was shocked when she turned up pregnant, and I didn't...uh...handle it well. But I'm here to get her now."

"Get who?"

"My daughter."

My eyes narrowed. "Tell me her name."

Kenny looked panicked for a moment, and I used my hold on his neck to shove him toward the door. "Get the fuck out of here. Don't come back."

"I have a lawyer. He's gonna get a judge to order a paternity test."

I'd turned my back on him, but his words halted my steps, and I pivoted around. I wasn't sure what his rights would be if he was proven to be Corinne's sperm donor, so I probed a little more. "Why now?" I asked curiously.

"I just found out about her."

"How?"

"My deal"—he stopped suddenly, realizing that telling me his dealer was his source was probably a really stupid idea—"um...this guy we both knew. He told me about Laura and that some rich-looking chick was asking around about the baby's family."

And there it was...a rich chick.

"I found out who they gave her to and asked around about you."

Which means he'd looked into me and figured out I had money.

"What do you really want?" I sneered. "Stop acting as if you give a shit about my little girl."

Kenny blinked, and I could practically see how hard his sluggish mind struggled to work through his thoughts.

"I might be willing to give up my rights," he drawled as he shoved his hands into his pockets. "To, you know, give her a better life."

My jaw clenched hard as I silently seethed, doing everything in my power not to kill the fucker. "For how much?" I gritted out.

"A hundred grand."

That was all she was worth to him? How could he ask for so little? I would give every penny I had to keep my girls safe. But I was pretty sure this asshole was no threat, and after years of bailing out Laura, I was sick of my money going up someone's nose or through a needle.

However, I'd consult a lawyer after I took out the trash.

"Get the fuck out of here," I growled. "My baby girl isn't for sale. Stay the hell away from us, or you're gonna find yourself facing down with the Iron Rogues."

"We'll just see about that," he muttered before turning and practically running out of the shop.

I stood there for a minute, trying to calm the fuck down, but I was itching to go after the guy and put a bullet in his skull.

"Why don't you go call Nevada," Dahlia suggested softly.

Nevada was the club secretary, but he was also our lawyer. "Yeah," I muttered, turning around and marching back to my office.

After explaining the situation to him, he was silent for a few seconds, then grunted, "Honestly? Just pay the motherfucker."

"He won't come back for more?"

"I'll draw up the paperwork to sever his rights, and we'll get him to sign before you give him a dime. Legally, there will be nothing he can do after that."

"Doesn't guarantee he won't show up later and stir up shit unless I pay him again," I argued.

"Which is why you, Fox, Mav, and a couple of

other enforcers take the paperwork to him. Make sure he understands just exactly who he's trying to fuck with."

I mulled it over for a minute, then sighed. "Fine. Can you get me that shit today?"

"Yeah, it's standard stuff. Won't take me long."

We hung up, and I glanced at the clock, irritated as fuck to see that I only had ten minutes before my next client.

I needed to calm down, and I knew hearing Ellery's voice would take the edge off.

"Hey, you," she greeted softly, making me smile.

"Hi, baby. How're my girls doin'?"

"Great. We're headed to the library for story time."

"Jake followin' you?" I was never gladder that I had someone watching over my girls all the time.

"Yes." She giggled, and my lips tipped up at the corners in response. "As tempting as it is to earn a spanking, I won't risk our safety."

"Plenty of other ways to earn a red ass, baby," I growled, shifting in my seat because my pants had become uncomfortably tight. "Not really a punishment if you're begging for it, though."

Ellery gasped. "I don't beg," she protested.

I laughed. "Baby, that was absolutely the wrong thing to say."

"Why?"

"'Cause now I'm gonna have to prove you wrong."

"What time are you done tonight?"

I grinned at her eager voice, and my swollen cock became painfully hard.

"Two more appointments, then I'm coming home to my girls. Shouldn't be more than two hours, tops."

"Great. We should be home long before that, so I'll get dinner ready."

"Thanks, baby. See you later."

"I lo—um—I'll see you later," she fumbled over her words.

I was about to call her on what she'd been about to say when Dahlia rapped on my doorjamb and jerked her head toward my station. Now wasn't the time to get into that discussion anyway. I nodded and said goodbye to Ellery before greeting my client and getting to work.

I was just about to start on my last client a little over an hour later when Molly came rushing around the small wall separating the tattoo stations. She was holding her phone to her ear but pulled it away and handed it to me when I looked up. "It's Jake. You need to take this. Something happened to Ellery and Corinne."

My heart lodged itself in my throat, but I snatched the phone and croaked, "What happened?"

"Ellery is okay, but someone took Corinne."

A roar of fury exploded from my chest, and I jumped to my feet, running to my office to grab my keys while still getting the details from Jake. He gave me the intersection where Ellery was waiting. "I'm on my way back. Fucking lost the asshole around a sharp corner."

Molly had followed me outside, and once I hung up, I tossed the phone to her before riding out of there like a bat out of hell.

I couldn't stop thinking about the worst-case scenarios. Living without either of my girls was not an option.

It was most likely Kenny, and it scared me even more that he had her and was probably high as a fucking kite. When I got my hands on him, he was gonna beg me to kill him before I was through.

12

ELLERY

I sat slumped over the wheel of the SUV until I heard the familiar roar of Zane's motorcycle. Then I scrambled out of the vehicle, almost crashing to the ground because my knees buckled. But he jumped off his bike and caught me before I went down.

"It's gonna be okay," he promised, a thread of steel in his voice.

I shook my head, tears starting to fall now that some of the shock had worn off. "It's all my fault."

"You're not to blame, baby," he reassured. "I don't know exactly what happened, but I know you'd never do anything to put Corinne at risk."

I was relieved that he didn't think that I was responsible for Corinne's kidnapping, but it didn't ease my feeling of guilt. "He took her from the SUV while I was driving."

"Tell me. Any details you can remember will help," he urged.

I took a few deep breaths and nodded. "It all happened so fast. I had just pulled over to wait for the prospect to catch up to me. Corinne was sleeping, and I twisted around in my seat to watch the light because I would pull out onto the street again when it turned green. I heard a noise in the back but didn't realize what it was at first. By the time I turned around, the man was already popping the baby carrier out of its base. I couldn't unbuckle my belt and get out of the vehicle fast enough to stop him from taking her. He just tossed her into the passenger seat of his car and took off. Without even bothering to buckle her in, and an airbag only inches from our precious little girl."

"You were parked here when he took her?" he asked.

I pressed my hands against his chest to try to stop my trembling. "Yeah. That's how he got the door open." I wasn't happy about the feature that automatically unlocked the car when it was put in park. I'd been so focused on watching for the prospect that I'd forgotten to lock it again. After this, we either needed to find a way to disable it or get a new freaking car.

He scanned the area and pointed out a couple of cameras mounted on the building to my left. "I'll get one of the guys to work on getting the footage. Hopefully, they caught something that'll help us find Corinne before our sweet girl realizes she's not with you."

"The prospect took off after him." I blinked up at Zane. "Have you heard from him yet? Maybe he caught up to them."

He shook his head. "Sorry, baby. The kid called the clubhouse. He hit a curb taking a sharp turn about a mile away, and the bastard got away. But he had the plate number, which'll help."

My shoulders slumped. "If I'd just realized the prospect wasn't going to make the light, I could have slowed down and stayed at the intersection with him. Then I wouldn't have needed to pull over to wait for him to catch up, and that guy wouldn't have been able to snatch Corinne from the back seat."

"No, this is on the asshole who got my sister pregnant and then ditched her. He must have a death wish to snatch her from you like that."

My eyes widened. "You already know who took her?"

"I'm almost positive," he confirmed before telling me about the man who'd stopped by Iron Inkworks, claiming to be Corinne's biological father.

The thought of her out there with someone who'd been willing to sell her to us scared the daylights out of me. I'd only been in her life for a little more than two weeks, but I considered Corinne to be mine.

"I don't know what I'll do if something happens to her," I cried.

Zane stroked his palm down my spine. "Don't worry, baby. The entire club is working on figuring out where that bastard took our girl. He's not going to have her long enough to do jack shit."

"Our girl?" I echoed, tilting my head back to stare up at him through the tears streaming from my eyes.

He swiped his thumbs against the wetness on my cheeks. "She's just as much yours as she is mine."

"I love her so much," I whispered, starting to sob in earnest.

He tightened his hold on me. "I know you do, baby."

I sniffled against his chest and mumbled, "As much as I love you."

His fingers flexed against my back before he

leaned back to stare down at me. "Fuck, baby. I love you so damn much, too."

"Really?" I clutched at his biceps. "Even after I let that guy take our little girl?"

"I meant it when I said this wasn't your fault," he growled, brushing a lock of hair from my forehead. "I could've prevented this if I'd paid the asshole off or put him in the ground for being a possible threat to Corinne. So if you're gonna blame someone, then you need to hold me accountable."

"You couldn't possibly have known anything would happen to her," I disagreed, shaking my head.

"And neither could you," he pointed out.

"I suppose you're right," I grumbled. Some of my crushing guilt eased, but I knew it wouldn't disappear completely until we got Corinne back.

"You bet your sweet ass I am." He gave me a quick kiss. "It's not the right time, but when all this is over, you're gonna wear my vest and my ring. And you'll have my last name before our next baby is born."

I hated that it had taken something as drastic as Corinne being kidnapped for us to finally give voice to our feelings for each other. But I loved knowing that Zane wanted the same future with me that I was dreaming about with him. "I want all of that."

He brushed his lips against mine again. "Just got word your property patch was ready this morning. I shoulda had it before now, but I was focused on getting my girls settled into our new house. And with Sheila and Tank out of town, she didn't get to it until a couple of days ago. Already got your ring, though. It's waiting for me to slide it on your finger when we get home—you, me, and Corinne."

I looked forward to seeing what he'd picked out for me, but not until our girl was safe. "Thank goodness she likes to sleep in the car so much. Maybe she won't wake up before you get her back."

"Have faith in the Iron Rogues, baby. My club brothers will move heaven and earth to help me find Corinne, so it's not gonna be long at all," he assured me, placing his palm against my lower back. "C'mon, I need to get you to the clubhouse so you'll be safe when I get word on where our baby girl is."

He guided me toward the SUV, but I shook my head. Lifting my hands, I showed him how shaky they were. "I don't think I can drive. I'm too upset."

"Don't worry." He rounded the vehicle and opened the passenger door. "I'm gonna be the one behind the wheel."

"What about your bike?" I asked as he helped me into the vehicle.

"A prospect is driving Viper over. He'll ride it back to the compound for me."

His answer surprised me because I'd been with Zane long enough to know that nobody rode his bike except for him. But desperate times called for desperate measures, and I appreciated that he was making an exception to his rule for me. "Thank you."

"Anything for you and Corinne, baby," he murmured as he buckled my seat belt before closing the door and rounding the front of the vehicle.

As soon as he was inside, he pulled away from the curb and headed straight for the Iron Rogues compound. They had extra men at the gate, and I took comfort from seeing their familiar faces.

Wrecker waved us through before making sure the gate closed behind the SUV. A crowd awaited us at the clubhouse, several old ladies making a beeline for my door after Zane parked. They ushered me into the building while the men talked. I turned down Dahlia's offer for something to drink or eat and sat on the couch with my knees drawn against my chest.

Zane came to check on me a few minutes later. "You doin' okay, baby?"

"Not really," I whispered, shaking my head. "But don't worry about me. I don't want to distract you from what's important. Focus on getting Corinne back. I'll be fine."

"We'll make sure she's good," Molly promised him as she and Dahlia sat on either side of me, taking my hands in theirs.

Zane gave me a quick kiss, and then I watched him stalk away, praying that they'd find our baby girl before anything bad could happen to her.

13

WHISKEY

"He pulled into a shit motel a few miles up the road from where Jake lost him," Deviant told me, pointing at his computer screen. It was frozen on a shot of Kenny in the parking lot, holding Corinne's baby carrier.

Rage like I'd never known blew through me, and I spun around, putting my fist through the nearest wall. "Fuck!" I bellowed.

I squeezed my eyes shut for a moment, taking a deep breath, but only managing to calm down a mere fraction. When I reopened my eyes, I looked to my prez for permission.

Fox nodded. "Nobody fucks with the family of an Iron Rogue."

I nodded my thanks, then muttered, "Let's roll,"

before stomping out of Deviant's office at the club-house. Ellery was still sitting on the couch with Mav's and Fox's old ladies, so I hurried over and bent down to take her face between my hands.

"Got a lead, baby. Me and the boys are gonna go check it out. Don't know how long I'll be, so I need you to stay here, where I know you're safe."

Ellery's hazel eyes filled with tears, and her lip trembled, but she nodded.

I kissed her quickly and told her, "I'll call when I have news." Then I rushed out to the front of the clubhouse, where several of my brothers waited, ready to back me up.

It was getting dark when we rode up to the motel, but we didn't want the noise of our Harleys tipping Kenny off. Or anyone being able to point the cops toward a group of bikers after he disappeared. Although the chief of police was a friend, he wouldn't break the law for us. He did bend it on occasion, though.

We parked at the grocery store next door and made our way to the front office. Some of my boys spread out to keep an eye on the room doors in case Kenny made a run for it.

Deviant walked around the side of the building, and a second later, the lights in the office went out.

"What the fuck?" someone exclaimed from inside.

Knowing the cameras were now down, I strode inside and straight up to the counter. Before the pipsqueak on the other side even realized what was happening, he had a gun pressed to his forehead.

"Kenny Harrilson. What room is he in?"

"I-uh-I don't know," the kid stammered. "I h-have t-to look it up in the-um-computer."

"Unplug the camera," I growled.

He reached over to the wall behind him and grabbed the cord hanging down from the camera mounted in the corner by the ceiling. Once he'd yanked it out of the socket, I called back to Storm—our Road Captain—who was holding the door open. "Lights."

He shouted the same word, and a second later, the electricity came back on.

The kid blinked a few times, but then he went cross-eyed looking at the gun pressed between his eyebrows.

"Look it up," I demanded, gesturing to the computer with the barrel of my pistol.

The computer had whirred to life, so he cautiously turned toward it and typed in a password. A program opened, and he scrolled through a database for a moment. His eyes were filled with terror when he faced me again. His voice was weak when he explained, "There's no Kenny registered."

An idea occurred to me, and I grunted in disgust, "Try Laura Thomas." The sick bastard probably thought he was being clever.

"R-room-um 12."

Storm stepped inside and slammed a fat roll of cash onto the counter. "We were never here. And if word gets out that we were, you'll pay that back with your fingers, toes, and teeth. Is that clear?"

The kid nodded vigorously and tentatively reached out to grab the money. Once he had it in his grasp, he shoved it in his pocket and ran out the back door, shouting, "I quit!"

I rolled my eyes and followed Viper outside. We relayed the room information to the boys, then a few set up a perimeter while the rest of us quietly approached Kenny's room.

"I don't want to spook him with Corinne in there," I murmured. "Who the fuck knows what he'd do if he felt threatened and was still alone with her?"

Ice stood in the shadows by the front window, looking through the crack in the curtains. Then he melted into the darkness before appearing at my side a second later. "He's in the bathroom."

The disgust in his voice made me cringe. My guess was Kenny was either shooting up or beating off. I really hoped it was the former since my baby girl was in the room with him. Not that I wanted her around drugs, but at least if he was high, he'd be an easier mark.

"Corinne?"

"She's still asleep in her carrier. He set her on the table in front of the window." He glanced back at the pane thoughtfully, then looked at me and muttered, "It's unlocked."

"Does it open far enough?" I asked, picking up on his plan.

He nodded and reached into his back pocket, pulling out a multi-tool, then disappeared and reappeared in his former spot.

Slowly, testing for any sound if the metal was rusted or something like that, Ice began to ease the window open. Which wasn't easy from the outside, but he was surprisingly adept at breaking and entering for a loaded, former pro hockey player.

Kneeling in front of the door, I used a lock pick on the knob until I heard the click of the lock disengaging.

I stood back up and turned to see how far Ice had gotten. He was using his knife to slice through the screen, which made it easier for him to push the window open even more.

Viper stood behind him and suddenly put his hand on Ice's shoulder. Then he looked at me and cocked his head toward the room.

Shit. Kenny must have come out of the bathroom.

Ice placed his hands on the windowsill and leaned forward, testing the width with his broad shoulders. Then he eased the curtain to the center, as far as he dared before giving Viper a chin lift.

Viper held up his hand, showing three fingers. He lowered one, then two, and when he tucked the third into his fist, I kicked the door in just as Ice reached through the open window and grabbed Corinne, quickly pulling her out.

"What the fuck?" Kenny shouted as his hand reached behind his back.

"Try it and the first thing I shoot will be your dick. Small target, I know, but I never miss."

Kenny froze and contemplated his circumstances for a second before lifting his hands into the air.

Viper stalked over and yanked the gun from Kenny's pants, then removed the clip and emptied the chamber before tossing it on the bed.

I briefly tilted my gun toward the door. "Move," I snarled.

"Where are you taking me?" Kenny whined. He sniffed and glared at me with watery eyes.

"To our guesthouse," I grunted as he walked past me.

The motherfucker froze and looked at me over his shoulder, his face awash with fear.

"Heard about it, huh?"

"Call the police," he begged. "I'll confess everything. Just turn me over—"

I laughed harshly, without any real humor. "You really think you're gonna get off that easy? You scared the shit outta my woman and KIDNAPPED our little girl!" I was bellowing at the top of my lungs by the time I finished, and Maverick poked his head inside the room.

"Save it for the guesthouse, brother. Let's get the fuck outta here."

I considered putting a bullet in Kenny's leg, just to give myself something before I exploded, but then we'd have to carry his ass to the car, and Race would complain for days if any blood got on the carpet of his trunk.

"Move it," I growled, poking him in the spine with the barrel of my gun.

When we stepped outside, I spotted Ice off to the side, swinging Corinne's baby carrier from side to side.

"She started to fuss but went back to sleep when I rocked her."

I lifted my chin in thanks, because I couldn't get any sound out of my clogged throat. Picking up the baby seat, I gazed down at my sleeping princess, and my knees nearly buckled at the rush of relief that swept through my body.

"Whiskey." I turned at the sound of Maverick's voice and saw him jerk his head toward a truck that was just pulling into the lot. "Let's get you two home to your woman."

I followed him to the vehicle, nodding at Fox who was behind the wheel. Carefully, I opened the back door and buckled my baby girl into the base he'd already installed for when Molly had their baby.

After quietly closing the door, I tossed my keys to Viper and didn't bother to threaten him with dismemberment if he so much as scratched my hog. I didn't care about anything but getting our daughter home to her mother.

I BRUSHED the tips of my fingers across Ellery's forehead, pushing away wayward strands of hair. Damn, she was beautiful. And watching her lying on the couch with our daughter resting on her chest, both of them breathing deeply in restful sleep... righted something inside me. Leaving a feeling of love and contentment.

But it wasn't quite enough to wipe out the rage burning in my gut. I needed to get this shit over with so I could come back to my girls with nothing but our future in my mind.

When I arrived home with Corinne, Ellery had been beside herself. She'd clutched our little girl to her and sobbed into my chest as I held them both. I hated to wake her, but I didn't want to leave without letting her know.

"Ellery," I whispered, running the tip of my digit along her soft cheek. "Wake up, baby."

She stirred, and her arms tightened around Corinne for a second, before relaxing again. It would be a while before either of us was comfortable letting Corinne out of our arms.

"I need to take care of some club business. A couple of prospects will be outside keeping watch, but I want you to lock up and set the alarm after I leave."

Ellery's brows drew down, and worry crept into her hazel orbs.

"Nothing dangerous, baby. Just business. I'll be back soon."

"Okay," she whispered.

We'd talked a lot about our life together, and she'd accepted that there were things I would have to keep from her from time to time, but only if it was club business. And though I didn't say it out loud, shit like tonight. That darkness would never come near her.

"Love you, baby."

"Love you, too."

I kissed her forehead, then brushed my lips over the fuzzy little head of our daughter before standing. Ellery cradled Corinne to her chest as I helped her stand, then she walked me to the door.

"Won't be long," I told her again. "Lock up, baby."

When the door was shut and I heard her set the alarm, I lifted my chin at the car across the street and received a wave in return.

As expected, one of my brothers had dropped off my bike, so I stalked to the driveway and climbed onto it. I sent a text to Mav, letting him know I was on my way, then I took off.

He was waiting outside the guesthouse when I arrived. It was a small structure built at the back of the compound, surrounded by trees so it was virtually hidden if you didn't know the place was there.

There were several "guest rooms," as we jokingly referred to them. A few functioned as cells, and two others were set up for interrogation. The one where Kenny waited for me was completely soundproof and easily sterilized since it was usually very messy when in use.

Mav unlocked the door and gestured for me to enter first. Then he locked it behind us and followed me to the basement.

Kenny was strung up in the center of the room, and I narrowed my eyes when I saw his split lip. No one was supposed to touch him. I scowled at Mav, and he shook his head. "Fought us getting in the trunk, his face hit the lid. Now get this shit over with so I can get home to my old lady." He walked to a chair in the corner and plopped down on it.

There were very few rules when it came to the use of this building, but one that Fox never budged on was using it alone. Just to make sure no one did anything truly stupid or fucked up, at least two of us always had to be in the room.

I faced Kenny, and he stared at me with stark

terror on his face, and his already wet pants grew darker as the smell of urine permeated the room. I grabbed a pair of gloves so I wouldn't get my hands soiled.

"Please," he begged. "Just turn me over to the cops."

"Rotting in prison is too good for you," I grunted as I strolled up to him, then I punched him in the nuts. "Death is too fucking good for you, but I'm not one to prolong torture." My right hook smashed into his jaw. "Well, not for too long."

———

SOFT HANDS GLIDED around my torso and clapped together on my chest just as I felt Ellery's cheek resting on my back.

Her curves pressed against me, and I sighed at the warmth of her body and the heat from the water cascading down over us.

"You're back," she whispered.

I took her hands in mine and raised them to my lips, kissing each one before turning around and taking her into my arms. "Sorry if I woke you, baby."

After returning from the guesthouse, I'd gone straight to the bathroom, put my clothes in the trash, and got into a steaming hot shower. I needed to wash away the filth before I climbed into bed with my woman.

"Don't be. I'm always happy to find you naked in the shower," she teased, rubbing herself up against me like a cat.

"Watch it, baby. Or you're gonna end up against that wall with my cock buried inside your pussy. And I don't have it in me to be gentle tonight."

"Who says I want gentle?" Her gaze dropped to my chest, and she traced my tattoos for a few seconds, then she looked up at me through her lashes. "I need you to make me forget."

An hour later, we collapsed into bed, both of us exhausted and completely satisfied. But I needed to do something before we fell asleep. I rolled over and opened my nightstand drawer, then picked up the little black velvet box I'd stashed in there.

Turning back over, I flipped the lid open and withdrew the three-carat diamond engagement ring I'd ordered for her. Then I tossed the box onto the ground and shifted onto my side to face Ellery. She mirrored my position, and her cheeks turned pink as she watched me take her hand and slide the ring onto her finger.

"Not gonna ask you to marry me because you don't have a choice," I said gruffly.

Ellery giggled, and my lips curved up.

"But I'll ask if you can be ready to do it this weekend."

She gazed at the ring for a few beats, then she shuffled over and pushed me onto my back before straddling me. "I'll marry you whenever and wherever you want. All I need are you and Corinne."

I curled up into a sitting position and cupped her beautiful face, memorizing every little fleck of brown and green in her hazel eyes. "I love you, Ellery. More than I ever thought possible. You and Corinne are everything to me."

"Me too," she whispered sweetly.

I kissed her hard, then grasped her hips and raised her up before plunging her back down onto my long, thick rod. "Now, let's get back to working on making more little munchkins."

The following morning, Ellery woke up and bolted for the bathroom.

I hoped this one was a boy. I needed someone to help me protect my beautiful girls.

EPILOGUE
ELLERY

Zane had proven to be every bit as overprotective as his club brothers. Between Corinne's kidnapping and my pregnancy, every caveman instinct inside him had been triggered. He barely let us out of his sight for the first few weeks following everything that had gone down, and he'd only gotten a little better as more time passed.

It had been another month, and today was the first time Zane had left us alone for more than a couple of hours. And I used "alone" loosely since a prospect had stayed on the front porch while he was at Iron Inkworks. But at least Corinne and I had gotten to stay home instead of hanging out at the tattoo shop while he was working.

"Hey, baby, I'm home," he called when he walked into the house.

"Did you hear that, sweetie? Daddy's home," I cooed to Corinne.

We were on the floor while she did tummy time, and even though I wasn't too far along in my pregnancy, I knew to wait for Zane to help me up. "We're in here," I called.

He strode into the family room, his lips curving into a satisfied grin when he spotted us. "There're my girls. I missed you two."

I rolled my eyes with a laugh. "You were hardly gone long enough to miss us."

"Wrong," he growled, crouching down to press a kiss to my lips. "It happens every time I walk out the front door. Doesn't matter if I'm gone for five minutes or five hours. I'm already looking forward to getting back to you before I pull out of the driveway."

"Aw," I sniffled. "Stop being so sweet, or you're going to make me cry. You know how easy that is with the pregnancy hormones coursing through my body."

"Your gorgeous-as-fuck body that's just getting better with you carrying my baby." His hand cupped my still-flat belly. "I'll try my best, but I'm makin' no promises. You deserve all the sweetness in the world since that's what you give our daughter and me."

I giggled at how easily he accepted my excuse, reminding me of the conversation Molly and Dahlia had back when I was first getting to know them. It was amazing how many things could be blamed on pregnancy hormones. And how many ridiculous food requests I could make even before the food cravings had kicked in.

"Did you remember to pick up pickles for my grilled cheese sandwich? And that yummy popcorn with the pink Himalayan salt that I've fallen in love with?" I asked.

"Of course, I did, baby," he confirmed with a grin as he lifted his arm to show me the bag he'd been hiding behind his back. "Got you some chocolate caramels too."

"Ooh, gimme," I squealed, reaching out to snag the candy and pop one into my mouth. "Yum."

"See, munchkin. Daddy did good," he murmured as he lifted Corinne into the air to nibble at her belly. "And when you get big enough, I'll bring treats home for you too."

"I'm sure you will." I beamed a smile at him. "You're such a good daddy."

He flashed me a satisfied smirk. "I sure as fuck hope so since we're gonna have a bunch of kids."

"A bunch, huh?"

"Yup." He set Corinne back on the floor. "That's what you want, so that's what I'm gonna give you."

"Lucky me."

He shook his head. "Nah, I'm the lucky one, baby."

He claimed my mouth in a deep kiss, and I whimpered when it was interrupted by the ringing of his cell phone.

"No," I cried as he pulled away to answer.

I couldn't hear what was said on the other end of the line, but I knew it was serious when every hint of good humor was wiped from his expression. When the call ended, he tucked the phone into his pocket.

"Sorry, baby. Gotta go." He brushed a quick kiss against my lips before explaining, "Some girl just called the clubhouse. Ice was in an accident."

"Some girl?" I echoed, my brows drawing together. In all the months Zane and I had been together, I'd never seen Ice with a woman.

"No clue who she was, but it sounds bad." His lips pressed into a grimace. "Blade's on his way to meet him at the hospital, and he asked for some help getting Ice's bike back to the club's auto shop. I'm gonna meet Wrecker and Wolf there to give them a hand since we're closer to where it happened."

I'd been looking forward to a quiet night at home with him, but one of the things I loved most about Zane was his loyalty to the people he cared about. So I pasted a smile on my face and nodded. "I understand. Please let me know if there's anything I can do."

"You can curl up in our bed and get some rest." His hand dropped to cup my belly. "You've got your hands full enough between taking care of Corinne and giving me another baby."

"Go." I patted his butt as he turned, earning me a hot look over his shoulder. One that I was sure he'd make good on when he returned home.

EPILOGUE
WHISKEY

The new apprentice at the shop was a pretty boy, and I had serious doubts about making it through his prospecting period. And he sure as fuck was too good looking to be sitting behind the counter with that shit-eating grin aimed at my wife as soon as we walked in.

"Hey, y'all," he said in a smooth Southern drawl.

Ellery, of course, smiled politely as she always did. She was too damn nice for her own good.

But this little shit had to know his place.

I took Ellery's hand, making sure he could see the big ring. I followed that up by putting my other hand on her belly—the one filled with my baby. Then I twirled her around so he could see the property patch on her back.

"Hey, prospect, did you clean my booth?" I barked.

His eyes snapped to mine as he swallowed hard. "Yes, sir. Are you expecting a client?"

"No, I'm going to use it to fuck my wife, now get the hell out."

Ellery gasped, her body shrinking against mine.

The new kid blinked hard but didn't say anything as he rushed out of the shop.

I gave him a wave before locking the door, then tugged Ellery along to my station. "Don't worry, I'll clean up afterward."

"Zane," she hissed but didn't release my hand or stop me once I got us in the space where I tattooed clients.

"Did you see the way he was looking at you?" I growled.

Ellery rolled her eyes. "Oh, come on, no one is looking at my pregnant body, especially not when we already have three kids at home, and I'm wearing your property patch and this."

She held up her hand, the diamond sparkling between us.

I took her fingers, kissing each one. "I'm looking at this beautiful body, and I know that damn prospect was too. So he needed to know that you're mine."

Before she could respond, I captured her lips, tasting her sweet gasps as she moaned into my mouth. Sliding my hand down the front of her dress, I could already feel the wetness pooling between her thighs as soon as I got to her silk panties.

Not wanting to waste another minute without being inside her, I pulled her toward the black, cushioned tattoo chair.

Trailing my lips down to her ear, I whispered, "Bend over for me like a good girl, baby."

"Zane," she breathed but didn't protest. She gripped the chair arms as I scooted behind her, running my fingers down her dress before hiking the soft material around her waist.

Crouching down, I easily pulled her wet panties to the side before I put my lips to her swollen pussy. She gasped, spreading her legs even farther, giving me access to the prize that I'd never get enough of, no matter how long we were together.

A few swirls of my tongue, and she was already coming, letting me lap up her sweet essence.

But I wasn't done there.

I'd almost been tempted to let that kid stay and make my baby scream loud enough to let that little fucker know she was mine. But nobody had ever heard her come other than me.

Standing, I undid my belt buckle and jeans, letting them fall to the ground before I gripped her waist.

"Hold on tight, baby," I growled.

Like a good girl, Ellery did as she was told, her hands going around the leather of the seat as she pushed her ass closer to me.

Sliding into her warm and waiting pussy was like coming home, and I instantly growled, feeling her tighten around me.

"Yes, Zane, you feel so good this way," she murmured.

The sound of our skin slapping together echoed through the empty studio, and I pushed harder, each thrust bringing me closer to the brink.

But I wasn't going to go before my woman.

Reaching between us, I circled her clit with my thumb, her wetness coating my fingers as she writhed against me.

"That's it. Come for me. Scream my name. Tell me you're mine."

I thrusted harder as she squeezed her tight pussy, massaging my dick.

"Yes, yes, Zane," she screamed.

"Fuck, yeah. Take my cock, baby. Milk it."

"Give it to me," she begged, gripping harder onto the chair and pushing back against me.

"That's my good girl," I growled as she clenched my cock, coming hard around me.

I followed soon after, shouting in ecstasy as her muscles rippled around me, prolonging my climax.

When I could finally catch my breath again, I grabbed some of the towels from the stack under my work table and knelt to clean her up.

"Feel better?" she teased with a big smile.

"I don't know, maybe I should remind us who you belong to one more time," I drawled as I pushed to my feet.

Ellery giggled, and I smiled. "I love you, Zane Whiskey Thomas," she whispered.

"Love you, too, baby. Let's go get our munchkins and go home."

My wife glanced around and frowned. "Don't you have a client?"

"I'll reschedule." My tone turned gruff when I added, "First I'm gonna tell that little shit with the wandering eyes to come back and scrub every inch of this place again. With a fucking toothbrush."

Curious about the girl who called about Ice's accident? Find out what happens in Ice!

And if you join our newsletter, you'll get an email from us with a link to claim a FREE copy of The Virgin's Guardian, which was banned on Amazon.

ABOUT THE AUTHOR

The writing duo of Elle Christensen and Rochelle Paige team up under the Fiona Davenport pen name to bring you sexy, insta-love stories filled with alpha males. If you want a quick & dirty read with a guaranteed happily ever after, then give Fiona Davenport a try!

Printed in Great Britain
by Amazon